A Will

of

Her Own

Linda Fisher

Mary, thank you for your unfailing encouragement. I value your friendship.

I hope you enjoy this trip to London with Lucy and Will —

Love,
Linda

Royal Fireworks Press

Unionville, New York

Library of Congress Cataloging-in-Publication Data

Fisher, Linda C., 1945-
   A will of her own / Linda Fisher.
       p. cm.
   Summary: In London in 1589, fifteen-year-old Lady Lucinda Culpeper,
   dressed as a man to try to fulfill her dream of becoming an actor, joins
   Will Shakespeare in investigating the murder of a servant girl and a plot
   to kill Queen Elizabeth.
       ISBN-13: 978-0-88092-640-9 (lib. bdg. : alk. paper)
       ISBN-10: 0-88092-640-6 (lib. bdg. : alk. paper)
       ISBN-13: 978-0-88092-641-6 (pbk. : alk. paper)
       ISBN-10: 0-88092-641-4 (pbk. : alk. paper)
       1. Shakespeare, William, 1564-1616--Juvenile fiction. 2. Great Britain
   --History--Elizabeth, 1558-1603--Juvenile fiction.   [1. Shakespeare,
   William, 1564-1616--Fiction. 2. Sex role--Fiction. 3. Actors and
   actresses--Fiction. 4. Spies--Fiction. 5. Murder--Fiction. 6. Great
   Britain--History--Elizabeth, 1558-1603--Fiction.]   I. Title.
   PZ7.F5334Wil 2006
   [Fic]--dc22
                                                          2006002900

Royal Fireworks Press
First Ave, PO Box 399
Unionville, NY 10988
845 726 4444
FAX: 845 726 3824
email: mail@rfwp.com
website: rfwp.com

ISBN: 978-0-88092-640-9 Library Binding
ISBN: 978-0-88092-641-6 Paperback

Printed and bound in the United States of America using acid-free paper, soy-based inks
and environmentally-friendly cover coatings by the Royal Fireworks Printing Company
of Unionville, New York.

PART
I

LONDON April 23, 1589

This shortcut was dangerous, but I was in a hurry. How many fifteen-year-olds could claim to have an audition at one of London's leading theaters? I gripped the hilt of my sword and ran to keep pace with my older, longer-legged cousin.

All around me, the square was teeming with seedy, smelly, scoundrelly men—men I would not stand next to in a theater's cheap-seat, groundling pit. The flea-infested tents along the walls held goods I would not waste a glance on, much less a farthing. As I ran, I turned to Thomas and cupped a hand over my mouth. Onstage, he would have called my question an aside.

"Thomas, have you noticed something about this part of the city? Even the vermin are heavily armed."

He cut his sea-green eyes toward me. "Are you admitting you don't have the equipment to take care of yourself?" He grinned and let his gaze wander down my frame that was smaller than his, shorter by at least three hands and different in other ways, too.

"Not at all," I said. "*This* more than makes up for any *equipment* I may lack." I slapped the hilt of my sword. "But I have no time to stop for a sword fight."

"If you do," he said with a shrug, "consider it a rehearsal. You never know. You might be asked to demonstrate your fencing skills. Weren't you the one who remarked that your entire future depended on a single performance?"

"Well, yes," I said, "but..." and then I stopped. Two men blocked our path, folding their arms and staring us down. They were both broad-shouldered, though neither was as big or as brawny as Thomas. They smiled at us, but without humor, like dogs.

As if on cue, both men placed their hands on their sword hilts, and a peculiar thing happened: the crowd backed away from the four of us. In the middle of that bustling square, I suddenly had all the room I wanted. But I was not worried. Not for nothing was my cousin Thomas nicknamed *Bernard,* after the fiercest animal at the Bear Garden.

I sidled toward Thomas, closing my fingers around the grip of my own sword. Some men, I knew from experience, were not happy unless they'd had a fight before breakfast. These two had a mean and hungry look. They took a step forward, and the taller one propped his elbow on the other's shoulder, aiming a blunt finger at us. Thomas and I did not budge.

"Good gentlemen," this fellow began, "my brother and I are lost. Might you kindly..." Abruptly, he broke off and glanced at his companion, who was plucking at his sleeve.

"Now, now, Patrick," this second one said. His eyes ran up and down the length of us, taking our measure, like a tailor or a coffin-maker. "You presume too much. How do you know that these two citizens here be *good gentlemen?"*

"A mere courtesy, Jack," the one called Patrick replied. "By callin' them good, I might incline 'em toward answerin' my question."

Thomas stifled a yawn. "And your question is..." he asked.

I glanced up at my cousin. So far, he seemed amused. For myself, I was in a hurry to get to my audition. I might never get such a chance again.

"If you please," Patrick said, "we'd like directions to the bull-baitin' arena."

The one named Jack nudged him in the ribs. "So, Patrick, are you thinkin' these two gentlemen might know a thing or two about the subject of *bull?*"

"If so, he's right," Thomas spoke up, with a laugh. "When the light is good, I am able to distinguish between your average Englishman...and a bull's *droppings.*"

This made both brothers grin. "Oh, well," Jack began, "as for that..."

"But," Thomas broke in, "with someone like, say, your *low-born Londoner,* the task becomes more difficult."

Jack's grin disappeared.

"Oh, I agree," I joined in, not wanting Thomas to have all the fun. "With such a specimen, you would need a torch light to see the difference. Most likely, though, you'd just set fire to his alehouse breath."

"Or to the lice in his hair," Thomas added. "But then he'd be all set for his supper...roasted meat."

At the word "lice," Jack's sword was out of his scabbard, giving Thomas barely enough time to arm himself. For myself, I could spare their fight only part of an eye and a parcel of an ear, for my sword was busy conversing with Patrick's. The crowd generously gave us more room, and the square soon echoed with clanging blades.

It may sound odd, but I feel most alive with a sword in my hand, not for killing, of course, which I have never done, but for the *poetry of the blade,* as Thomas liked to say. In a manner of speaking, my cousin Thomas adopted me. He's taught me everything I know. Everything that matters, anyway.

Years of following him around the streets of London had taught me how to size up opponents quickly. As the dregs of London, these two brothers may have been peerless, but as swordsmen, they were merely fearless. There was no grace, no strategy, no technique, only *parry-and-lunge* or *lunge-and-parry.* There was, therefore, the greater danger that Thomas and I could be killed. And death was never the aim of street duels such as this, nor even injury, but only sport. I hoped these two brothers played by the same rules.

"To the first blood?" Thomas called out to Jack. It was a standard question in London, to which the answer was always "yes," though my street duels thus far had never resulted in blood, *first* or otherwise.

"It'd be a bloody shame to stop there," Jack said, lunging at him with a twisted smile.

I should not have found time to see that strange smile. Patrick's sword sliced the air alongside my ear, and I leaped back, flat against a brick wall. The only bare brick wall in the square, and I had found it. Patrick was perhaps a step and a half away, and I had run out of room to retreat. Blue eyes agleam, he bared his jagged, yellow teeth. He did not have the look of a man who would stop at first blood.

"Wake up, laddie," he purred softly. "Are you dreamin' that a constable will happen by and save your scrawny neck? 'Twill not be happening, my lad. Not today, of all days."

"Oh, this cannot be a dream," I answered. "In my dreams I *never* smell horse piss." I finished with a well-delivered gob of spittle. It landed on his shirt front.

"Damn you," he said, taking a step toward me and then a mincing half-step.

What happened next only confirms the Biblical commandment against cursing. While he took the time to speak those two syllables, I, smaller and shorter dropped to the street and scrabbled away on the cobblestones. His blade slammed into a brick, and the tip broke off. Now his weapon was jagged like his teeth. He whirled toward me in a rage, but I was ready, executing a neat compound riposte and ending with my blade under his. I thrust him away and leaped to one side. From a distance of five or six feet, we assumed the stance and studied each other. Behind me, the swords of Thomas and Jack clanked and clinked against each other, sharp instruments making strange music. Over everything was the buzz of the crowd. "Thomas," I called out, not taking my eyes from Patrick's. "We must hurry. I have to be there at eleven."

"Goin' somewhere?" I heard Jack ask.

"Actually," Thomas spoke up, "my friend must see about a job."

My foot slipped against a rough stone, and Patrick darted forward. My blade met his at the last possible second. I had never fought a street duel with an opponent so much taller and heavier, and a shadow of worry entered my mind. With our blades still crossed, we leaned into each other, close enough that I smelled the garlic on his breath. The look in his eye troubled me.

"Blast you," I hissed. "We've never met, but you seem bent on drawing my blood."

"Oh, not just to draw some blood, laddie." His lips curled into a sneer. "I aim to kill you."

"Kill me?" I felt like an idiot repeating his words, but they were such idiotic words.

"Aye," he said, "and soon."

We continued to stand with swords crossed, pushing against each other, more like statues of swordsmen than live duelists.

"But why?" I whispered.

"Rosemary," was all he said, and then he thrust me away, but only far enough to make an attack.

"Rosemary?" I echoed, hoping to prolong my life.

He shook his head. "I've already said too..."

"Aiyee! Patrick!" a voice behind us cried out, as if in agony, and Patrick's eyes widened.

"Jack?" he said and spun around.

Jack lay on the street, clutching his bloodied arm, and Thomas was backing slowly away from him. It seemed like the right time to move. The next instant, I was at Thomas's side, the point of my sword aimed at Patrick.

"Constable!" someone in the crowd shouted. "Constable a comin'!" Then we heard the same cry from outside the square.

Patrick sheathed his sword and made a half-bow in my direction.

"Till the next time, laddie," he said, rushing to Jack's side.

When the constable finally arrived, I heard his huffing voice, but Thomas and I were already in the next street. No one else was in sight, and we ran until we reached the corner. Thomas turned to the left and slowed to a walk.

"Follow my lead," he said.

I nodded.

"Did you ever see those two men before?" he asked.

"No."

We were passing by a glover's shop and fell silent as a man and a woman neared us. Thomas touched his cap in greeting and paused to let them enter the store. I lifted my hand to do the same and noticed my hands were shaking. I glanced up at Thomas. His hand on his cap was shaking like mine.

Thomas is never afraid, I thought in alarm. *Never.*

"Thomas," I said. "Back there, why did you..."

"I had to. He meant to kill me." He shook his head. "I've never had to draw blood like that before."

"The same thing," I replied.

"Nobody's ever tried to kill me in a street fight," he said, rubbing his forehead. "These things are always just for sport. You know that. That's why I never worried about letting you..."

"Thomas!" I gripped his wrist, determined to stop his interruptions. "I know. I almost got killed just now. Thomas, you saved my life."

For the first time since the fight, he actually looked at me.

"The one called Patrick," I said, dropping his wrist and placing my hand over my heart. "He was ready to run his sword through me, right here. He said, *I aim to kill you.* And he would've, too, if you hadn't drawn blood from his brother."

Thomas looked at me in disbelief. "We encountered two bloodthirsty swordsmen at once? That makes even less sense."

"Maybe they were drunk," I said with a laugh. It felt good to be alive and laughing. "I asked Patrick why he wanted to kill me, and all he said was the one word, Rosemary."

Thomas cocked his head. He mouthed the word *Rosemary*. "Are you sure?"

"As sure as I am there's an England."

His eyes took on a faraway look. He seemed to stare right past me.

"You may be right," he said, "about the drunkenness. It was a very bad part of London we were in. Like as not, they had just stepped out of some alehouse. But," he went on, gripping my shoulders, "they proved one thing. They proved you were convincing as a young man. Here, look at yourself."

He turned me toward the glass front of the glover's shop. No wonder I had fooled Jack and Patrick. I looked nothing like the prim and proper Lady Lucinda Culpeper.

In the glass, my dark blue eyes glowed with excitement, tendrils of my light brown hair escaped from the boy's cap pulled low over my forehead, and my slim figure filled out the tunic and leggings I had borrowed from one of our servants. A thick vest and a purely decorative codpiece completed my disguise. Thank God for the codpiece. Some say it will soon go out of fashion. When it does, I may have to become a female full-time.

"When I dress like a boy," I said, "people take me for one. They always have."

"Because you're a good actress," Thomas added.

"Actor," I corrected, with more heat than I had intended. I threw his handsome face a smile and pushed some wayward hairs back under the cap.

The English stage did not allow actresses, which was why I was dressed as a boy for this audition. Truth to tell, I spent most days dressed as a boy. My father's big, lonely house is deadly dull for a girl my age—for a girl of any age. Father expected me to be content with embroidering handkerchiefs, but my years of following Thomas around London had given me an insatiable appetite for adventure. That appetite now led me to the theater where he once worked. Ironically, because of my size, if I were hired, my first role would probably be that of a woman.

A sudden movement on the other side of the glass caught my eye. A young woman about my age was arranging a pair of small, white gloves in the display area. She was dressed in the latest English style. A ruffled, white collar framed her face. Her blue, brocade dress fit snugly down to her waist, but the full skirt jutted out stiffly from her hips and fell to the floor in pleats and tucks and drapes. I did not realize I was staring until I saw her blush and turn away shyly. Thomas pulled on my sleeve.

"I think you convinced her, too," he said. "She believes you're a young man."

He set off down the street, and I hurried after him.

"I just wondered how I'd look in that color," I lied. "For a minute there, I forgot how I was dressed."

"You'd better not forget again, not if you want to fool my friends. Let's go," he said, picking up his pace, "or you'll be late for your audition."

I ran to keep up with him. He would never understand my real reason for staring into the glover's shop. I had seen a woman standing behind the girl, probably her mother, and the two of them were laughing about something. They

11

seem so comfortable, I thought, talking and laughing easily with each other. *Is that what mothers and daughters do?* I watched my brown boots kick up dust in the street.

"Thomas," I called out, "did you have any duels in France? Did you see any new fencing moves?"

"I wondered when you'd get around to asking me that," he said. He shook his head in amusement, but he began telling me about the balestras and stoccatas he had seen. I half-listened and lengthened my stride.

It was only two weeks ago that Thomas returned from France where he had been sent on family business. If I were a man, I probably would have gone to France with him. Unlike most families, unlike, say, the family of the glover who owned the small shop where we had just stood and gazed at our reflections, our family's day-to-day work involved rather more significant concerns. The men in our family dealt with the very life and death of our Queen. Because she is the subject of much undeserved hostility and because she has no heir, her Secretary of State, Sir Francis Walsingham, must spend most of his time searching for traitors. He depends heavily on my father, Lord Edward Culpeper, and Thomas's father, Lord Robert Blount.

Lord Robert is married to Father's sister, Rebecca, but Aunt Rebecca is not Thomas's mother. His mother died when he was an infant. This means that Thomas and I are not truly related, but we have always thought of each other as cousins—and so we are.

My father has risen to become one of the Ministry's most capable operatives. I should note that any acting skills I may possess have likely been inherited from him. (I cannot say what I may have inherited from my mother. She left this world as I was coming into it. I have only two things to remind me of her: a locket Father gave me which contains a small ringlet of her dark hair, and a pair of onyx earrings which I took from Father's study.) A church bell rang out, startling me from my daydream. "Run!" I said, racing past Thomas. When the bell rang for the eleventh time, we had just reached the entrance. Thomas looked me up and down and tucked some strands of hair under my cap. A chain loosely held the two halves of the wooden gate together, and we slipped inside, under the shade of a gallery. Dumbstruck, I stared at the seats near us and at the enormous stage less than fifty feet away. A few men stood or sat on it, no doubt rehearsing for the two o'clock performance. Even though I had been to this theater dozens of times and should have felt completely at ease, I prayed my audition would be in private. The fight with those pestiferous swordsmen had set my nerves on edge.

"Come on. We're late," I whispered, grabbing his arm. He did not move.

I dropped his arm and tried to step past him. He blocked my way. "Remember," he said. "Hold a man's gaze while you're being introduced." I nodded, impatient to be on stage. He only folded his arms. "And before you begin your speech, take a deep breath."

"Thomas, I'll remember!" I said, flaring my nostrils and sighing dramatically. "I'll remember everything you taught me." My anger did not make him budge an inch.

13

"You realize Mr. Bright could not promise he even has an opening?"

"I know, Thomas."

"Are you sure you're ready for this?"

All at once I understood the reason for his behavior.

"Thomas, you sound as if you don't have any faith in me. Don't you think I can do it?"

"I believe you can, Lucy. I mean Luke." He corrected himself with a grin and a shake of his head. "Otherwise, I wouldn't risk letting you make a fool of me in front of all my friends here. I also believe you really want to have a career as an actor. I'm just not sure you're doing this for the right reason."

I stared past him at the stage. My words poured out in a rush, words I had never spoken aloud, not even to Thomas.

"Oh, my reason is the right one. It's the best. I'm trying to save my life. I'm already fifteen. In a year or so, Father will marry me off to a man I'll probably loathe. I think he's had the fellow picked out for some time, his assistant in the Queen's ministry, Lord Winter." When I said his name, a shudder ran down my spine. I pictured the pale, self-assured face of Henry Rendle, the young Lord Winter, and shuddered again. Being in the same room with the man made me ill. What would the marriage bed be like?

"Your father wouldn't—"

"Oh, yes, he would—and that's exactly why I've never let him know how I feel about Henry. Father would force

14

me to marry the slimy fellow just to spite me. I think he wants someone who'll break my spirit." I turned to look into Thomas's uncommon, green eyes. "But if I had money of my own …"

And then I gave him my biggest smile. "Come on, Thomas. We're late." I shrugged. "Like I said, it's only my whole future that depends on this audition."

Grudgingly, he followed me. John Bright, the silver-haired owner of the theater, recognized Thomas before we reached the groundling pit, calling him by his old nickname of Bernard. I knew who Bright was, of course. Over the past few years, I had seen him and most of the other men here in many productions. I had seen the productions so many times, in fact, that I had been able to memorize the plays I liked, and even some of the ones I didn't.

Also on the stage with Bright were Robert Taverner, Gilbert Dereham, Ben Underwood and a few other minor actors. Quickly, Thomas introduced me to the others, and I held each man's gaze while his name was being said.

I then noticed another fellow onstage who seemed to be asleep. He sat off to the side, with his longish black hair hiding his face and his boots resting on a tabletop that was covered with a bright red cloth. Old Nathaniel, my father's servant, would have said the man was drunk. It was Nathaniel's opinion that actors stayed drunk. Like many Englishmen, including my father and Thomas's father, Nathaniel deemed actors dangerous folk. Understandably, Thomas had never told anyone in our family (besides me) about his stint with this acting company. Children of spies become very good at keeping secrets.

Just then, Thomas rested one hand on my shoulder and cupped my chin with the other. He aimed my face at Mr. Bright, as if I were a cow at auction.

"Young Luke has little ambition and even less skill, sir. Therefore, he has decided to become an actor. He wishes to begin with a leading role, of course."

Mr. Bright never got a chance to answer, for Robert Taverner grabbed my wrist and glared at me. He was a popular actor in his early fifties with leonine features and white-streaked, blond hair that fell to his shoulders. His most famous role was as the Mongol conqueror, Tamburlaine, and he seemed still to be in that imperious frame of mind.

"Young man," he growled, his blue eyes only inches from mine, "you'd better re-think that decision. Actors and their ilk are all rascals. The London Council says so. It must be true."

"Yes, that's a fact," Mr. Bright said agreeably, "but we like official pronouncements like that. When the Council made that statement again last week, we sold out all our performances."

"Right," Ben Underwood joined in. "And most of those tickets were bought by Puritans who wanted to judge for themselves about the wickedness of theaters."

"Thank God for the Puritans," Taverner said, clasping his hands together as if in prayer. I thanked God that Taverner had finally let go of my wrist.

So far, I had not actually said a word nor had I been able to. *Is it always like this,* I wondered. Actors seemed to like to hear themselves talk. Thomas, at least, tried to steer the conversation back to my audition.

He inclined his head toward Mr. Bright and spoke in a low voice. "Luke is an accomplished swordsman, sir, and a graceful dancer."

Before Bright could respond, Taverner was in my face again.

"Young sir," he hissed, "we are a wicked lot. We pray daily that the Puritans will preach against us on Sundays. It pads our pockets. Well, no one says it better than our Queen," he added and pulled himself up to his full height of six feet two. "'No amount of ordinances,' Her Majesty says, 'will keep a Londoner from enjoying himself.' She's right, of course. And she rightly intends for the government to profit from those enjoyments."

For a moment there was silence, as usually follows any public reference to our good Queen. It's as if people want to chew up what's been said, to see if there's any taste of treason to it, before they swallow it and go on.

Mr. Bright finally walked up and dismissed Taverner with a wave of his hand. "You always have the last word, Robert, and it's usually someone else's word. Hard for any-one to come onstage after the queen, isn't it?"

I had been thinking the same thing and wished that Taverner had not mentioned Her Majesty just yet. I wanted my reference to Her Grace to be the first.

17

Mr. Bright rubbed his chin and angled his head at me. "Give us an idea of your abilities, Luke. Recite something, anything you want." Accustomed to immediate obedience, he took one of the chairs that had been pushed under a table, turned it around and sat in it so he could rest his arms on its high back.

Just like that, he had ordered an audition. The others pulled up their chairs, too. Thomas folded his arms and gave me a smile of encouragement. I hesitated only long enough to step to the next table, where the sleeping drunk had propped his feet. Quickly, I lifted his boots, snatched up the red tablecloth and gently dropped his feet back to their resting place. As I tied the cloth around my neck for my costume, the man raised his head, shook back his black hair and aimed his dark, penetrating eyes at me. The small, golden hoop that hung from one ear made him look more like a pirate than an actor.

"And who do you think you are?" he asked in a deep voice that must have carried to the farthest row. "The king of hearts, all garbed in red?"

"Actually, I'm a queen," I said.. "And who might you be? Prince of pirates, I suppose."

I did not wait for an answer, though. I had an audition to give, and I leaped onto the table to stand beside his boots. After all, my whole future depended on this performance.

CHAPTER 2
A DUEL

I turned my back on the obnoxious pirate-actor and heard his feet drop to the floor with a thud, one heavy boot and then the other. He moved noisily from the table where I stood and then he joined my audience, leaning against one of the stage pillars and staring at me with unreadable eyes.

With the red tablecloth blousing over my figure, I was obviously portraying a woman. With my first three words, the who and where would become apparent: Queen Elizabeth, addressing her troops at Tilbury just before last summer's victorious battle against the Spanish Armada. To Londoners like me, her voice had become as familiar as the city's church bells. I took a deep breath, hoped Bright would think my imitation of Her Royal Majesty a good one, and began:

My loving people,

We have been persuaded by some that are careful of our safety,

To take heed how we commit ourselves to armed multitudes,

For fear of treachery. But I assure you, I do not desire to live

To distrust my faithful and loving people. Let tyrants fear. (When I said this, I raised my voice and my right arm.)

I have always so behaved myself that, under God,
I have placed my chiefest strength and safeguard
In the loyal hearts and good will of my subjects;

And therefore, I am come amongst you, as you see, at
this time, (These words required a sweeping hand gesture
to include everyone.)

Not for my recreation and disport, but being resolved,

In the midst and heat of battle, to live or die amongst
you all,

To lay down for my God, and for my kingdom, and for
my people,

My honor and my blood, even in the dust. (Expression
of English grit and determination here, in my face and
voice.)

I know I have but the body of a weak and feeble woman,

But I have the heart and stomach of a king,

And of a king of England, too, and think foul scorn that
Parma or Spain

Or any prince of Europe should dare to invade the borders of my realm. (It's tempting to overplay these last lines, but, then again, how does one overplay Queen Elizabeth?)

To which, rather than any dishonor shall grow by me,

I myself will take up arms, I myself will be your general,

Judge and rewarder of every one of your virtues in the field. (In the final lines, I remembered to break my voice.)

I know, already for your forwardness, you have deserved rewards and crowns;

And we do assure you, in the word of a prince, they shall be duly paid you.

My audience paid me with a loud hurrah, less noisy than the one given our good Queen, no doubt, but I was pleased. Thomas grinned wide enough for a saucer to fit in his mouth. He stood and led the applause while the booted, earringed pirate studied me. I did not give him more than one or two glances during my performance, but it looked as if he had been cleaning his nails with the point of a small dagger.

Mr. Bright approached me as I jumped from the table. Only now did my chin begin to tremble, and I bit the inside of my cheek.

"Very impressive, lad. Delivered with skill and emotion. While you were performing, you bore an uncanny likeness to our monarch."

My chin relaxed a bit. The question of salary flitted through my mind.

21

"Unfortunately," he went on, with a shake of his silver locks, "our company has a full slate of actors at the moment. Alas, I could not even re-hire your cousin Thomas if he wished to return to our troupe."

He paused to throw Thomas an apologetic smile, and I felt a tear well up in my eye. *Blast!* I thought, willing the tear to dry. A girl would cry. I refused to cry. When Mr. Bright turned back toward me, my gaze was hard as steel.

"Just three weeks ago," he went on, "I hired another actor to take Thomas's part. Our London season will run only another month. As you probably know, our schedule is like all the other theaters. We have two weeks of perform- ances, with a different play each day, and then we start again. At the beginning of this season, we engaged a young man somewhat like you in appearance to play most of our female roles." There was a sound at the rear of the stage, and Mr. Bright looked up in surprise. "In fact, here he comes now."

I followed his gaze, eager to see the young man who played the roles I coveted. He did indeed look somewhat like me. The boy was dark-haired and clear-skinned, with strong, handsome features that would show up well even to the back of an amphitheater. He was dressed in the latest fashion, and I took him to be a member of the upper class, just like me, until he opened his mouth.

"Sorry to be late, Mr. Bright. It's all my sister's fault, and my mother is making me loony."

His voice was high-pitched, and his accent was educated, but merchant, rather than upper class. I guessed he was from Southwark, across the Thames, and decided that if Mr. Bright really preferred this boy's voice to mine, then I might never get a job with this company.

"You're not late, Arthur," Mr. Bright said, motioning to me as if he intended to introduce us. Before he could, Arthur halted about ten feet away and put the back of his hand wearily to his forehead.

"My sister is missing," Arthur said, "and my mother's worried sick. She wants me to spend every wakin' moment lookin' for Sally, but I can't. I just can't, and Mother doesn't understand that. Anyway, Sally'll come home in a day or two with a big story that Mum'll lap right up."

Where Thomas is concerned, my senses act like a cat's whiskers. Even before he moved, I knew he was very upset. He marched up to the boy and grabbed his arm. "You say Sally's missing? You've had no word from her at all?"

I stared at my cousin in amazement. Who was this girl named Sally, and why was Thomas in such distress? Arthur tried to pull his arm from Thomas's bear-like grip.

"Uh, well, no," the boy said. "I mean, yes. We haven't heard from her, and that's what worries Mum. I try to tell her Sally's a big girl. Sally and I are exactly the same age, and I certainly don't come home every night."

Robert Taverner spoke up, his thick, gray eyebrows bristling. "How can you and your sister be exactly the same age?"

Arthur giggled and I realized why Bright had selected him for female roles. "Why, we're twins, of course, and that makes my mother think I ought to be more...sympathetic. Mum has this idea that twins are closer to each other than ordinary brothers and sisters. Well, the old girl won't admit it, but Sally and I are very different, and we've never been particularly clo..."

"That is incredible," Taverner interrupted again. "I have never heard that twins could be of the opposite sex. I've never known any twins except the 'boy-and-boy' or 'girl-and-girl' variety."

Perhaps because he was an actor, Taverner was accustomed to holding forth at center-stage, but I wished he had not broken in just as Thomas was questioning Arthur. My cousin shifted from one foot to the other so often that one might have thought there were anthills on the stage. It was apparent to me that he had pinned his hopes and his heart on this girl named Sally, who was now missing. In the meantime, Arthur seemed to prefer dealing with Taverner's digression instead of Thomas's distress.

"Nevertheless," the boy went on, his eyes moving warily from one man to the other, "Sally and I are living proof that it happens. You can ask my mother," he added.

"We can do better than that, Arthur," someone said in a sarcastic tone, and we all turned to the rear of the stage.

The man standing at the doorway was the actor I recognized as Gilbert Dereham. I had always considered him the weakest member of this troupe. If I had weighed two hundred pounds more and possessed a prodigious mustache,

I would have tried to persuade Mr. Bright to give me Dereham's place in the company. Dereham pointed to the surly player who at this moment was leaning against one of the stage pillars, still cleaning his fingernails.

"That gentleman can vouch for the truth of your statement," Dereham went on. "I say, Will, you can settle this disagreement?"

The man he spoke to looked up with an expression of mild interest. When he raised his eyebrows, like a king giving a subject permission to speak, I realized I had seen this fellow before today. In the past three weeks, I had seen him in several plays at this theater. So this was the troupe's newest member, Will Somebody-or-other.

"Yes?" The fellow's voice betrayed irritation.

"Tell Robert here how you know that twins can be of different sexes."

"Since you already seem to know the answer, Gilbert, kindly tell everyone else. It will be more dramatic that way, like a Greek chorus informing the audience, so to speak."

Gilbert turned toward us as if deflated, as if Will had taken all the fun out of it. "Well, you see, Robert, it's like this. Will has children of his own back in what is the name of that small village you come from? Stratford, is it?" He gestured toward the subject of his story but got no help. Gilbert's enthusiasm was waning fast, yet he plodded on, moving slowly toward his audience while he explained. "Anyway, two of the children are twins, are they not? A boy and a girl?"

"Yes," Will said, and then in an aside, added, "but only two."

John Bright spoke up. "Ah, yes, I remember you told me about them. The boy has the same name as that character in Thomas Kyd's play. Hamlet, wasn't it?"

"That's close, sir. His name is Hamnet. Judith is his sister."

Taverner snapped his fingers. "Will, what was the name of that play, the one..."

But Thomas could stand it no longer. "Arthur," he said sharply, "come outside with me. We must talk. Now."

Turning on his heel, he headed to the door at the rear of the stage. Meekly looking to Mr. Bright for guidance, Arthur followed Thomas, but dragging his feet. I, on the other hand, was reluctant to stay. *Should I go with Thomas,* I wondered? With a stab of something like jealousy, I realized that he had not asked me. *Who, I asked myself, is Sally? A new girlfriend?* Thomas never spoke of her.

"What's he doing now?" Dereham muttered. "Sticking his nose in where he isn't wanted. The man's like a pirate stealing a woman somebody else saw first."

He stood just at my ear, but was oblivious of me. His angry tone was so unexpected that I wondered who on earth he was talking about. Did he mean this man named Will who resembled a pirate? I followed Gilbert's hard gaze and saw that he was speaking of Thomas.

"Damn him!" Gilbert cursed under his breath. "The *hoi polloi* of London may have liked the upstart well enough, but they have no taste."

Usually I don't presume to correct another's mistakes, but Gilbert Dereham had earned a comeuppance. No one was going to criticize Thomas while I was around. "You said that wrong." I spoke slowly and evenly, determined to make him look at me. It worked.

"What do you mean?" He twirled his thick mustache with ring-studded fingers.

"*Hoi polloi* in Greek means 'the masses.' Using the word 'the' is redundant."

"And which university did you attend, *mon enfant?*" he asked. Abruptly, he moved, almost on tiptoe, to the door at the rear of the stage and stood there, as if eavesdropping. I wished I could be a fly on the wall or on Dereham's large rear end to hear Thomas and Arthur.

Taverner spoke again, undeterred by the interruptions. "I say, Will, what was the name of that old play about twins? You know the one. It was by Terence."

"Robert," Will said, shaking his head very deliberately and staring at the older man in puzzlement. "I do not know of any play that Terence wrote about twins."

Robert threw him a look of utter disbelief. "Why, man, we've talked about it before. In fact, you told me you were writing a modern version of it. Surely, if you plan to steal from the play, you know the name of it."

27

"Yes," Will said with a laugh, "but I always improve upon my thefts." He rubbed his chin. "There is an old play about twins, Robert, a Roman play, but the playwright was Plautus, not Terence. I can't believe you've forgotten the name. Why, you must have performed in it a hundred times when you were a boy."

"Of course, he did," Ben Underwood broke in. "In the very amphitheaters of Rome. And in the original Latin, too."

Taverner's grin was an easy one, as if this sort of raillery only served to demonstrate his elevated status in this company. He turned toward the empty theater, gripped his lapels and addressed his remarks to the expensive seats. "I think that jealousy always cheapens the truly professional actor."

Dereham came forward from the doorway. "Latin? Did someone mention Latin?"

I saw Underwood throw a grin and a quick wink to Mr. Bright.

"Gilbert," Underwood said, "Taverner wants our troupe to perform a play in Latin. What do you think of that?"

Gilbert pulled on the tip of his long mustache. "Brilliant. We'd set London theater on its ear. Which play? One of the classics or an original? I'm something of a writer, myself, you know, so I'm game. What about you, Underwood, you're a university man. You'd be up to it. And you, too, John," he said, smiling at Mr. Bright. He aimed a penetrating gaze at Will. "What about you, Will? How's your Latin?"

Will put a hand at the base of his spine and bent double as if in pain. "Oh, it's not well, Gilbert. I think I sprained it last night."

Underwood and the others laughed, but Gilbert turned red and scowled.

"What I meant was how well do you understand Latin?

"Oh, if she is like most women, Gilbert, then I do not understand her at all."

"You know perfectly well what I..." Gilbert began, but the laughter of the others drowned him out.

"Gilbert, don't talk nonsense," Taverner said. "And you know perfectly well that the London public loves our good English words too much. They won't come to see a play in Latin. Why, man, that would be as unheard-of as having women act in our plays."

I felt myself turn red at this last remark. I was grateful that all eyes were on the two men at centerstage.

Gilbert laughed out loud. "You could not be more wrong, Taverner. Having women act in our theaters would be a sacrilege, a horror. But staging a play in Latin would be marvelous, a triumph for intellect."

Taverner shook his mane of silver hair and rolled his eyes. "Now, listen, Gilbert. Enough of this. All I want is the name of that Roman play about twins. Do you know the name of such a play?"

Gilbert's face turned red. "No, but I..."

"Why, Robert," Will broke in, "I would be willing to wager that even this *boy* knows the name of that play you are talking about."

Then I saw that his gesture meant me.

"Well, boy," Will continued, aiming the point of the knife at me. "What do you say? Your cousin Thomas seems to think highly of you. If the future of the English stage is to rest on your narrow shoulders, surely you must know something of dramatic history. What is the name of that ancient play about twins? Come, come," he said, snapping his fingers imperiously. "Your reputation is dying even afore 'tis made." He put his hands on his hips and rocked back and forth on the balls of his feet, his black eyes laughing at me all the while.

I cleared my throat. The man's cockiness riled me. And all this time I had thought he was drunk.

"As every pit-faced groundling knows, it was *The Brothers Menaechmi,*" I said, as casually as I might say hello.

"Aha!" Taverner cried out. "Now I remember. *The Brothers Menaechmi.* That's right. You didn't really expect him to know that, did you, Will? Here you are! Made a fool of by a young boy. Who would have believed it?"

The others in the room laughed. I stared at Taverner in admiration. Few people are able to divert mockery away from themselves like that. Only a moment before, he had been the object of laughter, but now Will was the ridiculed one. Taverner moved away from us to lean against the table where he gave me a mock salute.

"Watch him, now," Taverner warned, pointing to Will who stared at me in silence. "He's composing a reply. Be ready to write it down for posterity. Ten syllables to the line, I'll wager, and all full of rhyme, no doubt."

A slow grin crept over Will's face. "No, Robert, I have no rhyme, not this time. The boy spoke true. Give him his due. But tell me, Luke," he said, catching me off guard again, "like the saint whose name you bear, do you always tell the gospel truth? Are you, in other words, an honest man?"

What did he mean? Had he seen through my disguise?

"I'm an honest person," I blurted out. "I'm as honest as the next man." I cut my eyes toward the door. Where was Thomas?

Will glanced around the gathering. "Well, let's see. It looks as if I'm the man closest to you. That makes me the next man, doesn't it? Are you, say, as honest as I am?"

"How should I know?" I said defiantly. "I don't know you."

"Well, that's true. None of us really knows another person, do we?" He grinned and slapped the flat blade of his dagger against his palm, as if for emphasis. "For instance, we don't know you at all. Your cousin, though, is willing to vouch for you, and he claims that you would be a great addition to our troupe." He continued to hold my gaze with his dark eyes. "You fence, I believe Thomas said."

Self-consciously, I rested my hand on my sword hilt and then quickly made a fist instead. "What are you getting at?"

31

"Only that you have a sharp mind. Is your sword as sharp?"

I glanced around. Were fencing matches always this easy to come by?

Robert Taverner rose from his slouch and strode toward us.

"Thank you, Robert," Will said with a curt nod, "but you won't have to act as my second. This is just a friendly little sword fight."

Taverner snorted in disbelief. "Serving as your second was never my intention. I only wanted to stop this mischief at the outset. Leave the boy alone, Will. He merely answered your question. He means no harm."

"And I also mean no harm," Will said with a smile of total innocence. "Just that while we're all assembled, and there's ample time before today's performance, we may as well complete the audition."

The smile disappeared instantly, and he turned to Mr. Bright.

"With your permission, John?" Will asked.

With a broad grin, Bright settled himself into a chair once more. Actors, like musicians, seemed always ready to play.

"If Luke is agreeable," he said.

But no one else gave me a chance to agree or disagree. The others joined Bright at the table as spectators, and Taverner leaped forward.

"Then I'll serve as judge," he said. "Let's see...three hits wins, all right?"

32

"But wins what?" I asked Will. "Mr. Bright has told me there are no openings in the company now, so what will our little exercise be for? We must make it worth our time."

Worth our time, indeed, I repeated to myself. An idea was taking shape. I held Will's dark gaze.

"Interesting idea," he said. "What shall we wager? Not money, I think. Money seems a little too commonplace for someone like you."

"Ah, but you don't know me at all, sir. You said so yourself. You are right about one thing, though. Money is rather dull, especially old money. Let's wager a favor, instead. A kind of boon that the loser will grant to the winner."

"Such as?"

"Oh, surely, there's some task that you need to have done, something that you don't want to do on your own?"

He snapped his fingers. "There is something. It requires a middling sort of intelligence. There is the matter of copying some pages which I have written. Are you able to read, Luke? Can you copy what you read?"

"I can copy as well as the next man. I can copy as well as you." I paused a moment. "I can even copy Latin."

His face broke into a complete smile, making him look more roguish than before. "And the favor that you wish?" he asked, stroking his mustache.

"Write a role for me in your play, for next season," I demanded.

He raised his eyebrows. "But Mr. Bright selects the cast. What if you do not rightly play the role that I write in my play? Mr. Bright would be right to roll you out of here, would he not?"

"I told you to watch him," Taverner said. "See how he twists your words?"

I had already discerned that this actor named Will had no authority to help me win a job here, but I frowned and shook my head as if disappointed. The pretense came easily because earlier when Mr. Bright had genuinely disappointed me, I had pretended not to care. I am destined to become an actor, I told myself, and took a bold step forward.

"Then I have a question. How long a time do you estimate the copying of those pages might take?"

"Oh, not above two hours. That is, if you make no mistakes."

"Then my favor, if I should win the wager, is the same amount of time, two hours, to help me with a task that also requires a middling sort of intelligence."

"But what is the nature of this task? I do no larceny, petty or otherwise, and I perform character assassination only for cash compensation," he said, running his thumb across his fingertips.

"I assure you that the work is honest, that it may prove useful to you as a writer and besides," I added, mimicking his roguish smile, "is there any chance that my sword could prove sharper than your tongue?"

"Ha!" Taverner said, clapping his hands together. "Then the particulars are arranged."

I smiled to myself. Win or lose, I would have two hours of this handsome actor's time. But I was not going to lose.

"Ben," Mr. Taverner called out. "Bring us two foils, please."

Underwood brought two swords from the rear of the stage. His keen eyes flicked from me to Will, and his lips curled in anticipation. Taverner took the swords, examined the covering on their tips, and held them out to Will and me, with great ceremony.

"Tell me, Luke," Will asked, testing the heft of his foil. "Do you prefer the Italian style of fencing? Or perhaps your taste runs to the more rigorous Spanish fashion?"

"I prefer neither Italian nor Spanish, neither French nor Euclidean nor Moor," I answered, stretching my arms and legs with a lunge at a nearby pillar. "My style of choice is the mute, sir. I prefer to speak with my sword, not with words."

"But a sword can be made with words, can it not?"

"Ah, if one speaks to the letter and not the spirit, you are right." I lunged at the pillar again, and abruptly halted, locking eyes with him. "But mere words never draw blood."

"Touché," Taverner said, stepping between us. "Let us begin, before the stage is littered with whole alphabets of corpses."

"Will," Ben Underwood called out, leaning back in his chair and propping his feet on the table as I had seen this fellow named Will do only a little while ago. "You know it is entirely possible that you may be underestimating this boy. Have you had shrift lately for your soul?"

"No, but my sole aim is to make short shrift of this boy, as you call him. Besides," he said, with a sudden smile, like sunlight washing over a field, "I go to chapel every day, as you all do know. Sometimes twice a day."

"Ha!" Taverner shot back. "As we all do know, Will, that is only because you live on Chapel Street."

I took off my own sword, entrusted it to Mr. Bright to guard and examined the foil that Taverner had given me. After a few more thrusts and leaps, while Will warmed up in the same way, I was ready.

We fell to.

I had already noted the stage's construction, especially the placement of the two central pillars and the railing around the perimeter. It was the height of about two hands, and I knew I had to respect the boundaries of this arena.

As Thomas had taught me, I spent the first minute studying my opponent. While our swords clanged against each other noisily but harmlessly, I admired Will's physique. His shoulders, arms and legs were very muscular. In fencing, though, large muscles can hinder movement, and a foil is not very heavy. My own body is slim, strong without seeming so. Stamina counts for the most here, that and strategy. Will, I concluded, moved gracefully enough but with no particular finesse.

Even before I saw him lift a sword, I had guessed at his level of skill. He was no Londoner, after all, but came from the country town of Stratford. "Small village," Gilbert Dereham had called it. He had children. He was an actor with this company. And, according to Taverner, he was writing a play. I decided that he had most likely received his training in this sport relatively late in life. I, on the other hand, had been fencing practically since I could grasp a table knife, thanks to my cousin Thomas. I met Will's sword once again, mapped out my strategy and began to formulate my victory speech.

Footsteps sounded behind me from the rear of the stage, but I was far too well trained to turn in that direction. All my senses focused on my opponent.

"Good Lord!" a familiar voice shouted. "He'll kill him."

"Oh, nonsense, Thomas," John Bright called over his shoulder. "It's only a friendly match."

The skin on my neck tingled. What did Thomas mean? Who would kill whom?

Unable to stop myself, I half-turned to see my cousin's face. His mouth hung open, his eyes were wide with shock and, it seemed, genuine fear.

The doubt I saw in Thomas's green eyes, the smugness in Will's dark ones, the eyes of the other actors intently following our match—there were eyes everywhere I looked, and my concentration broke. Will rushed at me, and I parried his attack at the last moment.

Unbidden, the apt words of M. Roche, Thomas's old fencing instructor, came to mind: "He who would dare to win must do so with the eyes."

Will and I continued to lunge and parry, our foils whistling through the air or clinking against each other, and I resolved not to blink or take my eyes from his. Guarding the expression in my own eyes formed my defense. Guessing the expression in his formed my offense.

So slowly that he could not have seen my intent, I maneuvered our little dance toward centerstage. Back and back I pushed him, and I turned to let him push me. Then, to lull him into over-confidence, though he possessed enough for several men, I pretended to stumble. When he lunged forward, I dodged and caught him with my foil high on the shoulder blade.

"A hit for Luke!" Taverner called out. At close range, his diction was even more precise than it had seemed from the gallery.

I smiled. With part of my mind, I contemplated where Will and I would go during the two hours' time, where we should begin, where we might end.

Thomas clapped and shouted "Hoorah!" Behind me, a chair scraped the floor as someone jumped to his feet. Unintelligible phrases, hoots of encouragement and cries of astonishment filled the air.

And surprise filled Will's eyes. Determination firmed the line of his jaw. It occurred to me that perhaps I should let him have a hit, for his pride. He would be less sullen later, when he paid me his debt of time. It would be easy enough to arrange, I thought, as we moved back and forth across the stage. I could make a slower than usual sidestep, a clumsy parry, a...

He nicked me on the shoulder with his next lunge. His grin revealed even, white teeth.

"A hit for Master Will!" Taverner's booming voice rang out again.

"Now it's a real match," someone shouted.

Forget the mercy, I said to myself as we parried downstage. *Finish him off. Two swift strikes,* I thought, and then I would tell him the favor I desired. After that, Thomas and I would stay for the afternoon performance, and the three of us would begin to...

The scoundrel caught me just above the heart. A very pretty move it was, a riposte that even M. Roche might not have seen coming. I had not expected that he would know such a counter-attack immediately after a parry.

"A second hit for Master Will!" Taverner cried out. Already I was tired of his perfect articulation. "The score stands at two to one," he added, quite unnecessarily.

"Proportion, Luke," Thomas called out. "Remember the three." But someone else shouted just then and drowned out the rest of his words. I knew what they were, though. Proportion, distance, time, the honorable foundations of this sport. But they crumble to dust if you lose, and I was losing.

A whoosh of air beside my ear signaled the too-close blade of this man who was not nearly as skilled as I. Ha! If that were true, then how was he winning?

The eyes, again. The eyes! I had forgotten. Suddenly, I felt my guard, my resolve and my rhythm meld together in a surge of energy as we executed our unfriendly dance across the stage. I focused on his eyes, not on how dark or deep or long-lashed they were, but on how much of his game he gave away with them, how he unconsciously glanced in the direction of his next thrust. And I forced myself to betray nothing with my own eyes.

Mentally, I critiqued his pretty moves, and it came to me just how I would win. In a staged production, fencing requires such attractive steps as his, such choreography. The crowd demands beauty within its violence. *Well, pretty be damned,* I said to myself, and breathed a hasty prayer of thanks for my years of street-fighting alongside Thomas, of playing in any match, anywhere, anytime. I went on the attack—a brutal, proper, yet ugly attack. I watched his eyes, and I lied with mine.

My mind held no words but the silly couplet Thomas had taught me years before.

A laugh, a prank, a joke, a jest,
One and two and a third in your breast.

I touched him between his ribs, with a one-two-three, a compound attack that uses a feint disengage, double disengage and then the attack. He sprang back as if burned.

"A second hit for Master Luke!" Taverner yelled out in his sweet voice. "They are dead-even."

The tension in the room doubled, as if storm clouds crackled above us. The shouts of the others in the room blended into a single, incomprehensible roar. No longer did a smile play on Will's lips. Back I pushed him, back toward the pillar on the left. He had forgotten it was there. Only for a moment did he hesitate as his backbone brushed the post, but it was all I needed. There I struck the third blow as the childish rhyme pulsed through my blood. *...a third in your breast.* Had I said the words aloud?

"A hit!" Taverner shouted. "A very palpable hit for Master Luke."

From the commotion they made, the men at the table behind us seemed to have transformed into a gaggle of groundlings. Their loud whoops and footstomping rumbled across the stage. I was not looking at them but at Will, and just then he did the most amazing thing. With a look of shock, he slid down the length of the pillar, and a slow grin spread over his features. Nonchalantly, he laid the foil beside him and folded his arms behind his head, as if lying down for a nap.

I came to a stop in front of him. "Are you all right?"

"Fine. Just preparing to die."

"To die?" I repeated. "But I didn't harm you. This is tipped with a button." I twanged the end of the foil as proof."

"Ah, but you have irreparably harmed my good name. I have been bested by a boy, and the shame is too much to bear. The only thing worse would be to lose to a girl."

He shifted as if to find a more comfortable position, and I began to suspect that the man liked to hear himself talk

"The ancient Romans killed themselves, you know, whenever capture seemed imminent. Since you are a worthy opponent, I will allow you to complete the execution. Still," he went on with an exaggerated sigh, "a man's birthday is as good a day as any to die, don't you think?"

"So today is your birthday," I said. "St. George's Day, isn't it?"

"Yes, we share the same date, myself and Sanctus Georgius."

"The calendar is crowded with you saints," I said with a laugh. "I fear you may spend the entire two hours of the time you owe to me in talking nothing but nonsense."

He hit himself lightly on the forehead and leaped to his feet. "Of course! The wager! I forgot. How discourteous of me. Naturally, all vows of suicide are off for the day. My promise to help you takes precedence over any selfish desire to die honorably. And what is this favor you wish?"

Before I could answer, Thomas and the others walked up to us. Will laughed along with the others when they made fun of his loss to a mere boy, but I detected a strain

42

in his good humor. John Bright quickly put a stop to the foolery by ordering everyone into costume for the afternoon performance. They obeyed as if he were a general.

When the actors had left, Thomas grinned at me.

"Congratulations, cousin. You just proved you don't need my protection. I'll be off." He gave me a mocking salute and headed for the rear exit.

"But where are you going?" I asked.

"I need to find Sally." He threw the words over his shoulder. "Arthur told me some places she might have gone. A girlfriend's house in Southwark and a tailor's shop Lord Wotton sometimes sends her to." He turned toward the door again.

"Thomas! Wait." I ran toward him.

He glanced back impatiently, still retreating. "What?"

"Who is this Sally? I mean, who is she to you?"

He halted, his eyes narrowed. "A girl I met. A beautiful girl. I care about her. I have to find her."

I laughed, hoping to keep him here longer.

"What about Ellen? I'm finally able to tolerate her presence, and now you go off after some other girl."

He shook his head. "Listen, I have to go."

"Did you think I would lose?" I asked softly. "Just now?"

"Never."

"Then what did you mean when you said, 'He'll kill him'"?

He seemed to hesitate, but with only a few long strides, he was at my ear. "I looked serious, but you forget that I'm an actor. I said that for Will's benefit. It's something that men do, Lucy," he whispered, "just a scare tactic." He stood up straight and winked. "That's probably the reason you won."

"You know that's a lie," I shot back, angry he would joke about this. "I won because I remembered everything, everything you taught me. And it was easy. There at the end, I even thought of that old rhyme. Do you remember?"

I pulled my sword from its sheath and demonstrated my final lunge at Will.

"A laugh, a prank, a joke, a jest,

One, two and a third...

"In your breast," another voice finished.

I whirled around. Will stood at centerstage. The spot suited him.

"I have only a minute or two," he said. "My costume for today requires extra time. What is this favor you wish?"

Thomas gripped my shoulder. "I must be off, Luke." He left with a grin and a wave to both of us.

I waited till I no longer heard his footsteps. Thomas would not approve of this favor, even though I had his interests in mind.

"I want us to work together," I said, sheathing my sword and walking toward centerstage. "I want to find Sally, Arthur's sister. She's the girl who's missing."

"But why?"

44

"Because...she's missing, and my cousin Thomas seems to be in love with her. I'd like to help find her if she's all right."

"And if she's not?"

"We'll find that out, too."

"Why me?" he asked. "Why do you think I'll be able to help you find this girl? And why involve me at all? I've met her here at the theater a time or two, but I care not a whit about her."

"You seem very clever." His gaze was disconcerting. I shifted from one foot to another and crossed my arms over my chest. "Very observant," I mumbled. "Besides, it occurred to me that writers should be able to figure out things more easily than other people, because they understand human nature so well. Of course," I added, not wanting to over-inflate his sense of himself, "I don't even know if you're a good writer."

He nodded, and the dark eyes glowed like the onyx earrings that once belonged to my mother, the glittery ones I'd hidden in my bedroom.

"I've held several different kinds of jobs before," he said, "but I've never worked as a...constable."

"Well," I jumped in, eager to motivate him, "if you ever decide to put a constable into one of the plays you write, you'll know what the demands of the job are. When we look for Sally, we might need to locate a constable or two and you can study the breed." He still seemed unconvinced, so I thought fast and rambled on. "For instance, if most constables have fish breath or if they're pig-brained, you'll be able to write about them more accurately."

The jewel-like eyes gleamed. "My father is a constable."

"Oh," I said, in a small voice. "And, of course, he doesn't have..."

"No," he shook his head very deliberately. "No fish breath."

"And he's not..."

"No, he's extremely...clever. Just like me."

"Well, at any rate," I said, "that's the favor I wanted. I'll stay for the play. Maybe we could begin our search after that."

His gaze held me for a few more seconds. "This search for Arthur's sister seems to be like a lark to you, just an afternoon's entertainment like the play we're about to perform. Have you considered that it might be dangerous?"

"Does that frighten you?" Long ago, at my father's knee, I had learned that this question works wonders on the male animal.

"Ha!" He slapped his hand on the pillar that I had backed him against. "You return a question for a question. With a mind like yours, you should aim for the law, my boy, not the stage."

Abruptly, he stared at the floor and chewed on the inside of his lip. "I suppose I must agree to the terms of the wager," he said, in such a wounded tone that one would have thought the wager was over money instead of time. "After all, I promised. But only two hours. Not a minute

46

more. Time is money." Then he raised his dark eyes to mine. "And now I must prepare to earn some. Meet me outside the back door after the performance." He slapped the pillar once more, and I wondered if he wished it were my backside.

He had taken no more than two steps when I called out to him.

"I just realized something. You know my name, but I don't know yours."

He came to a halt and pivoted neatly on his heel. A smile lifted the tips of his mustache.

"Of course, Master Luke. That puts you at a disadvantage, doesn't it? Let me introduce myself." With signal grace, he made a low bow. "The name is Shakespeare," he said. "William H. Shakespeare. At your service."

CHAPTER 3
SEEKING SALLY

The audience turned a blind eye to the last-act trickery in the afternoon's performance of *The Mighty Myconides*. When Myconides descended from the heavens, everyone in the theater pretended not to see the ropes that lowered him from the hut in the ceiling of the stage. Cannonballs rolled across the floor of the hut, sounding like thunder, but really to cover the noise of the crane that operated the ropes.

Will, in the title role, acquitted himself very well, holding his own with Taverner and Bright. Few actors in London could boast that much.

As for Arthur, it may be that I'm jealous of the boy's good fortune. I could have done a better job with his roles, but the roles were partly to blame. The women he portrayed were weak and uninteresting. I've seen many English plays, but only a handful with strong female roles. Even the great Christopher Marlowe only depicts women who are in the shadow of a man. How odd in a country where our Queen is such a powerful force.

One unexpected event happened, but not onstage. Among the other spectators, I saw a familiar face. Two rows below me sat young Lord Winter, the very same Henry Rendle who worked for my father. Today, he was in disguise, dressed in the coarse worsted and dark brown apron of a butcher. I guessed he was following a suspect under orders of Sir Francis Walsingham. As the daughter of a spy, I am experienced at seeing through makeup and costumes, but it was Henry's flat, black eyes that gave him away. There is not enough makeup in London to hide those eerie orbs. I strenuously avoided his gaze.

When the performance ended, there was the thunk-a-thunk of apples hitting the stage. It's the final sound effect of modern plays and the one provided by the audience. The fewer apples, the more they had enjoyed the performance. Today's play earned only a half-dozen or so of the fruit. I shuffled outside with everyone else and waited for Will behind the theater along with half the female population of London. Of course, not all of them were hanging around to see Will. From their conversations, I gathered that some were waiting for Underwood, some for Dereham, and some were even hoping to see Robert Taverner, as old as he is. Shouts of excitement went up each time the door opened.

When Will finally came out, he smiled at the circle of women and girls who rushed up to him, but he kept walking briskly. When he drew even with them, he pulled a white scarf from around his neck and threw it up in the air, drifting down over their heads. You'd have thought it was a gold coin. He didn't even look back.

"Master Luke," he said, striding up and motioning for me to hurry. "How did you like the afternoon's perform-ance?"

"You must not be as popular as Taverner," was my only answer as I fell in step with him.

"Why do you say that?"

"Taverner also lost his doublet. By now, he might not be wearing a stitch."

49

"Hmm...the London public has absolutely no taste. Have you noticed that?"

"Gilbert Dereham said as much, but with more eloquence," I retorted.

We walked half a block talking in no loftier fashion. Finally, Will halted, folded his arms and stared at me.

"What is your plan? Two minutes of the two hours are already gone. If you're wise, you'll utilize my time better than this."

I folded my arms, trying to capture his gaze. He looked past my shoulder as if already bored. "As I see it, we have two choices open to..."

A shiver ran down my neck, and I slapped at what I thought must be a fly. Instead, my fingers closed around a slim wrist, and I whirled around to find myself looking into a pair of devilish, blue eyes.

"Ellen!" I cried, dropping her wrist. "I've told you not to do that."

"Oh, Luke," she said, with a shake of her long, blond hair. "You know you like it. You're just like your cousin. Where is Thomas, by the way? I waited outside the theater after the play, but he never came out. I've been following you ever since." She flicked an appraising glance at Will and then gave me a slanting smile. "If I didn't know better, I'd think Thomas was trying to avoid me. Do you know where he is?"

"He's been very busy lately, Ellen. I haven't really..."

"He's been seeing that tramp, that Sally Clopton, hasn't he?" She laughed, a nasty, humorless laugh. "There's no future in that. And then he'll come running back to me. He always does. Will you give Thomas a message?"

She took a step toward me, smiling slyly and looking at me from under her long lashes. The bodice of her green silk dress was cut low to show off her two greatest assets. Whenever she sighed, they rose like twin loaves of dough. Will, being a writer, might use a different simile. I noticed he noticed.

She sighed and rested a gloved hand on my arm. "Would you do that for me, Lukie?"

I cringed when she called me that. *Thank God she's never met me as Lucy,* I thought. *What pet name would she give me then?*

"Uh maybe, Ellen. Uh what's the message?" I took a step backward, aware that Will was taking all this in. Ellen can be as full of surprises as a cellar in the dark. I was glad Thomas had fallen in love with another girl, but I wished he had told Ellen.

She lifted a small drawstring bag that was tied to her belt. Taking out a folded, white cloth, she placed it in my hand and closed my fingers over it. "Give this message to Thomas," she whispered, holding my gaze. "Don't look at it or throw it away. Promise me that you'll give it to Thomas."

"I promise," I snapped.

"Thank you, Lukie."

Before I could pull away, she bent forward and kissed me on the cheek, then turned and walked slowly away, swaying her hips provocatively as if Thomas might be watching.

Will leaned close to my ear and whistled softly. "That's a very interesting girl...Lukie."

"I loathe her! You saw her come up behind me. Why didn't you give me a warning?"

He shrugged. "Actually, you can blame yourself for that. Recall our conversation about constables and fish breath and such? Your basic message was that writers should use every opportunity to study people. I decided to test the concept by studying you. I saw the girl come up behind you and wondered how you'd react. Now I know. By the way, when are you going to look at her message to Thomas?"

I tightened my grip on the cloth.

"I may not like Ellen, but I did promise her I wouldn't look at it."

"No, you didn't," he said smugly. "You only promised her you'd give it to Thomas."

"You're right! I did, didn't I?" I opened my fingers and unfolded the cloth.

"Anyway, weren't you curious?" Will asked. "Even if you did promise, how could you not read her message?"

"It's just a handkerchief. There's no mess..."

And then I saw it. I could tell Will saw it, too. He made a clicking noise in his throat and spread the cloth out across my hands to display it better.

In the center of the handkerchief, pricked out perhaps with a pin, were the words *I Love You.*

Only I don't think Ellen used ink. The words looked as if they were written in blood. Will whistled low under his breath. "There's a girl who makes a strong impression, don't you think?" He continued to stare at Ellen's backside.

"About as strong as a cartload of dung," I muttered, folding the cloth with its blood-red message and stuffing it into my pocket. Now I had no intention of giving it to Thomas, promise or no promise.

"What was I saying before she came up?" I asked.

"Something about: We have two choices."

"Oh, yes. We can go across the river to Southwark, to look for Sally at her home, or we can go to the house of her employer, Lord Wotton."

His eyes glinted with interest.

"I say we go to his lordship's since it's right here in London."

"Well, it may be," I said. "But that's the problem. I have no idea where he lives. As for the other option, Southwark is fairly small, compared to London, and we could probably find her family's..."

"I know where Lord Charles Wotton lives," Will broke in. "I've made it my business to know where the nobility live in London. I've gotten as far as Lord and Lady Wrangell, so we're in luck, alphabetically speaking. That is, if this is the same Lord Wotton."

I cocked my head at him. "What an odd hobby you have. Do you plan to rob their houses?"

"Each nobleman is a potential patron of the arts, Luke," he explained patiently. "I'm simply looking to the future. Besides, it's a way to learn the streets of London. Follow me, my boy. I'll lead you straight to Lord Wotton's."

And he did, setting a brisk pace through London's winding streets. I wondered if he had really gotten as far as Lord and Lady Wrangell. If he had, he might have seen Lady Lucinda Culpeper leaving the family home. And heaven knows how she might have been dressed!

As I had suspected, this actor named Will Shakespeare liked to hear his own voice. He pelted me with one question after another, often answering them himself, but throwing me an occasional dark glance to see how his answer played.

"Why did Mr. Bright refer to your cousin as Bernard?" he asked after we had traversed a block or two. "That's not really his name, is it? If I were guessing, I'd say it's because he bears a resemblance to the largest animal at the Bear Garden. Would the truth bear me out? What about your surname? Culpeper is a very...colorful name, isn't it?"

"No more colorful than Shakespeare. What kind of name is that?"

He chewed on his lip. He was leading me down Watling Street, near St. Paul's.

"Shakespeare," he finally said, "is the kind of name that causes fights in school when other children make fun of it. Shakespeare is a very fertile name, breeding nicknames like Shakes Beer and Shakes Pee-er. Children are tirelessly creative with unusual names."

I grinned in agreement. "Yes, I remember a time or two when I got called 'Culled-pepper' and 'Arse-wipe-paper.' Makes a person tough, doesn't it?"

His pirate's eyes gleamed at me. "It can turn a boy into a man, all right."

I changed the subject.

"Taverner said that you're writing a play. Does acting bore you already?"

We were passing a bookstall outside St. Paul's, and he paused a moment to look through a slim volume. Shaking his head at the vendor, he put the book back on the shelf and then motioned for me to fall into step with him again.

"I write for the same reason I act," he went on, as if no interruption had occurred. "To earn money. I have a family to support, as you know. In fact," he said, turning to me, "you've learned much more about me than I have about you. For instance, why..."

"This play that Taverner said you are writing," I broke in. "Have you a name for it?"

"Two names, actually. That's the problem. I can't decide between The Syracusan Twins and The Comedy of Errors. Which do you prefer?"

"Toss a coin," I said with a shrug. "Might there be a part for me in this play you are writing, this plagiarism of Plautus?"

He frowned and kicked at a rock in our path. Perhaps he wanted me to settle the problem of his title.

"Possibly. You and young Arthur resemble each other, as Mr. Bright told you. You and the boy could play the two Dromios or perhaps even the two chief characters, the Antipholus twins, Erotes and Sereptus."

"Arthur can have the smaller role," I said.

"There are no small roles," he said condescendingly, as if he had just invented the saying. "Only small actors."

"My, my," I said with an innocent smile. "What an interesting play you must be writing, if all the roles are leads. Tell me, Master Shakespeare, have any of your other plays been produced on the London stage?"

"No," he said, coloring slightly and waving his hand to dismiss the subject. "I wrote my first one last year, an exploration of love, but the experience was like...like a musician playing scales. I did it for practice, one might say."

"Perhaps it will be staged someday," I said, with an encouraging smile.

"I'm sure it will. Keep a lookout for it. *Love's Labour's Lost,* I call it."

Encouragement be damned! That was one thing this peacock did not need.

"Have, uh, have you actually completed this play?"

56

He gave me a sharp glance before answering. "Not quite. I'm still trying to work out some twists in the plot. With two sets of twins, it's a little hard to keep up with who is who from scene to scene."

I knew what he meant. Some days I had trouble remembering who I was supposed to act like.

"Some days," he said, "I think I get too caught up in the story I'm writing. He slowed his pace, talking softly, as if to himself. "I forget that life is not as malleable as art."

"What do you mean...malleable?"

He shrugged and threw a glance at our reflections in a storefront we were passing. "Sometimes I wish life could be as neat and tidy as art. At the end of a satisfying story, for instance, the wicked get punished, the good get their reward and, in a modern story, at least, the hero gets to kiss the pretty girl." He shook his head and gave me a too-bright smile. "It'd be nice if we could manipulate life that way, wouldn't it, Luke?"

"I suppose so," I said, trying not to stare into his dark eyes, trying to seem uninterested in the dark meaning behind his words.

Just then, we turned a corner and Will stopped, putting out his arm for me to stop also.

"Here we are," he said, in a tone that was almost reverent.

Lord Charles Wotton's London home is rather bizarre for a man of the British nobility. Will explained that the three-story, stone building had been designed by a student

57

of the Italian architect, Andrea Palladio. The name meant nothing to me, but I saw a definite Italian influence in the structure's columns, arches, and domed, central section. All at once, I realized that I had no plan for getting inside.

"What do you suggest?" I asked Will. "We don't even know if this is the right Lord Wotton. If you were writing this scene in a play, how would your characters get inside?"

We stood pondering the problem for a moment, and I studied his eyes that really were as dark as onyx. Years ago, I discovered a little-used bedroom on the third floor of our house, directly above Father's study. When I pulled aside a piece of carpet in one corner of the room, I could look down through a crack in the flooring and see the area around the fireplace. More than once, I watched Father interview spies there. I have seen Father open and close the safe that is hidden in the brickwork to the left of the mantel. This safe is where I sometimes availed myself of loose change, occasional pound-notes, and once, my mother's beautiful onyx earrings. By rights, they belonged to me. At any rate, they're mine now, and Father has never seemed to miss them. Until now, I had never seen anything as dark as those stones.

"We should go around to the rear," Will said abruptly, startling me out of my daydream.

"This way," he went on, walking quickly into the alley. "Servants are almost always ready to talk to strangers. Especially London servants. Anything to keep from working."

He knocked loudly on the back door. It was opened at once by a young woman with a worried, unwelcoming face that was surrounded by wisps of curling, red hair. The door was not overly welcoming, either, held in check by a sturdy iron chain. The woman said nothing, so Will attempted to fill the void.

"Good afternoon, miss. My companion and I would like to ask you a few questions about the whereabouts of a damsel who..."

The door slammed shut.

"Almost always ready to talk," I repeated and knocked softly three times. "Hello," I said through the door. "Sally Clopton is missing. Her mother's very worried about her. I'm Luke. This is Will. We need your help." Short, choppy statements, straight to the point, maybe even straight to this woman's heart. I'd soon see.

The door opened again, but only after she undid the chain, and then she flung it wide for us.

"Missin'? Sally's not missin'. I think she up and quit," the woman said, her face and limbs all atremble. "Just when his lordship's got a big party all set for tomorrow night, his first dinner party since his wife died last year, and Sally leaves me with everything to do by myself. And his lordship's not even here. Won't be back for hours. Humph!" She snorted in anger like the bulls I've seen at the bull-baiting arena.

"So Sally quit?" I asked, putting one foot on the threshold, but trying not to seem as if I were barging in.

59

"I s'pose she did. She hasn't come back to work since day before yesterday."

She turned around and threw her floured hands into the air to show us the kitchen and all the work that Sally had left behind. It was a huge kitchen, which made the woman look even tinier. The vaulted ceiling went up and up, strung like a tree at Christmas, not with candles but with pots and pans, clusters of dried herbs and woven baskets and spider webs. I wondered if the food here ever contained a clumsy spider. Vegetables filled a giant washtub on the central table. On another work surface, sprinkles of flour, a bowl of dough and a pan of pungent, spiced apples indicated that a pie was being contemplated.

"I got all the cookin' to do," the woman exploded. Her age was difficult to tell, with all her ranting, but she seemed to be about as old as Will. Freckles dotted the end of her nose. "And the cleanin' of this kitchen, too," she added, walking to a door on the opposite side of the room where a mop stood beside a couple of buckets. She grabbed the mop handle and gave it a good shake.

Will took that opportunity to walk past me into the kitchen and to follow her. "As my friend Luke said, we are looking for the girl. When we find her, perhaps she might come back to help you."

She whirled around, practically spitting out her words. "Help me? Why, she never did nothin' when she was here. Always runnin' around London town doin' errands for his lordship." The woman shook the mop again, this time in Will's direction.

He shrank from her anger, and I hid a smile behind my hand. Even when I had lunged at him with a foil, Will had not flinched as he did now. He stepped out of reach of her weapon and leaned against a wall on the opposite side of the room. He wore the look of a man who had eluded a mop before.

"I've never met Sally," I said, moving out of the doorway and into the room. Behind me the door closed softly. "But my cousin's in love with her. For his sake, I'd like to find her."

The woman stopped her fuming and stared at me. "Your name is Luke?"

I nodded.

"So, Thomas is your cousin, then," she said with her first smile.

I nodded again.

"Ah, Sally doesn't deserve 'im. She's a slattern." She wiped her hands on her apron.

"Well, you know how men are," I said. "How we men are." I fumbled with a button on my jacket. "A pretty face, a good figure."

"I thought you never met her." The maid's voice hardened.

"Oh, I haven't, but Thomas described her to me. She, uh, she's very pretty, he says, and..." I let my voice fade out, hoping that she would take up the thread of my meaning.

"Aye, that she is," the woman agreed. "But beauty don't get the housework done. Beauty's just an accident of nature, not near as useful as knowin' how to cook."

She went on to tell me about Sally, and I compared the picture she drew with the servant before me. Where Sally was tall and womanly, the maid in this kitchen was short, shorter than I am, and only a little bigger around than the mop handle she clutched. Where Sally had long, thick, wavy black hair, this servant's hair was fine, curled like ribbons and the color of strawberries, the same color as the freckles on her upturned nose. As she described how Sally's body affected the male animal, this woman's fair skin shone with energy, even through the layers of flour. She paced and fumed her way around the table and chairs in exasperation at what fools these mortal men be.

And then the back door opened, the one that this woman had opened for Will and me, and a stranger put in his head. Perhaps he had been on the receiving end of her mop before. When he saw that she was far across the room, he stepped inside. Just before he shut the door, a fat, gray tabby cat slipped in, and the man kicked at it without connecting. It darted to the maid's side, where it sat at her feet and watched the man suspiciously.

The stranger was tall and shaped like an enormous brick. The cut of his black coat and pants identified him as a servant, and the red vest showed him to be the chief servant of someone's household. Lord Wotton's, I wondered?

"It's possible."

"Of course, it is," he said, licking his lips and giving me a sidelong glance. "I've known many a young person who assumed a disguise to keep Papa from knowing what he did, or what unsavory characters he did it with."

I felt the need to change the subject.

"Do you think that Pettigrew, I mean Brooke, might be Sally's murderer?"

Will shrugged. "He could be. It's too bad we were interrupted just now. I was about to tell him that Sally was dead, just to see his reaction."

"No, you weren't. You were about to give him a scar on his cheek."

"Do you really think I would've done that?"

He licked a bit of cinnamon from his fingertip, quite pleased with himself.

"Who knows?" I answered. "As you said yesterday, no one can truly know another person. What I'm more interested in is why you went to Number Six Speight Street at all. Last night you told me that we should leave Sally's murder for the constable to investigate."

"And I believe that even more firmly today, but I was moved by the same pernicious urgings that made you follow me to Speight Street—*curiosity*. This card was our first real clue. Till we found it, you and I had been involved in an aimless way. As you may have noticed, I don't like to do things aimlessly. Now, can you guess why I wore a disguise this morning?"

123

"You didn't want anyone to see you enter a brothel."

"Very good!" He raised his eyebrows admiringly and popped the last bit of bread into his mouth.

"I guess a married man has to be careful," I added softly.

He winced slightly and wiped the crumbs from his mouth.

"Mostly I don't want my children to hear sordid stories about their father. But speaking of disguises, Luke, you really should think about wearing one yourself, at least once in a while. If you want to become an actor, my boy, you must learn to like disguises, to feel comfortable in them."

"Thank you for the advice, master." I came to a stop and made an exaggerated bow, a kind of disguise to hide my expression.

"Well, well," I heard Will say. "Look where we've ended up."

I wheeled around and saw the minarets of London's infamous Tower Prison.

At the sound of hoofbeats, we both turned. Two black horses plodded toward us, pulling a wagon.

Will whistled softly under his breath. "Not exactly the sort of thing you'd see in Stratford."

The driver wore the stony expression and the red jacket of a Tower guard. Standing upright in the back of the wagon was a hurdle, a kind of frame like a sled. A man was tied to it, with each of his four limbs secured to a corner of the hurdle. His wide eyes were fixed on the prison that loomed ahead of him, but I was close enough to read his fate in them, as if the judge's sentence was still

124

ringing in his ears. I'd heard the words often enough at public executions: "...to be hanged, cut down alive, his members to be cut off and cast into the fire, his bowels burnt before him, his head smitten and his body quartered and divided."

The wagon drew even with us, and a shudder zigged down my spine. When the horses turned onto the bridge over the Tower's moat, I took my first deep breath since we'd stopped.

"Tell me," Will said, "the hurdle always signifies an execution, doesn't it?"

I threw him a smug smile, glad to be the one with an answer for a change. "Always."

His face contorted as if in genuine pain. We walked in silence for a moment, aimlessly, it seemed to me, though I didn't care.

"What could've been his crime?" he asked after a moment.

I shrugged. "Usually treason. The sort of thing my great-uncle Thomas did, adultery with the wife of the king. Nowadays, it's usually plotting to assassinate the Queen."

"Strange as it may sound," Will said, angling his head at the gloomy Tower, "one of my chief goals in life is to stay out of that place."

I laughed aloud. "That shouldn't be too hard to do."

"You might be surprised. Many an English writer cuts his teeth on those bars. Our government distrusts writers, especially those who write for the theater."

I recalled last night's conversation I had overheard between Father and Thomas. Why had I assumed that Thomas joined the troupe to spy on actors? "But Will," I said, "Mr. Bright told me the London Council suspects actors of being troublemakers. He didn't mention writers."

"Tell that to all the writers behind bars. Writers are the really dangerous ones. They're the ones with the ideas, often revolutionary ideas. You don't work for our government, do you, Luke?"

I blinked. His question and his roguish grin startled me. "No, of course not," I said. And it was no lie.

He stopped to stare at the Tower, and I stopped, too. The wide, high entrance stood open like the mouth of a great beast. When Will spoke again, it was in a low voice. "Perhaps I can trust you, then. We consider ourselves free men here, Luke, but England is not truly a free country. We have no freedom of thought, no freedom of religion. The man who thinks about things must move very carefully."

He stroked his mustache.

"You're a native Londoner," he finally said, cutting his eyes toward me. "There's something I've been wanting to ask an authentic citizen of the world. You've probably heard of that pamphlet about Lord Dudley." He wrinkled his forehead. "I forget the name."

"Leicester's Commonwealth." I tossed the answer off, the way I'd said *The Brothers Menaechmi* yesterday at the theater. "Why?"

"I say, Alice, are you entertainin' a guest? You know Lord Wotton don't allow that." He looked at me, not at her, letting his eyes rest on my sword.

"They aren't guests, Basset. They've come to find out about Sally."

His thick, bristling eyebrows arched dramatically, forming a single line.

"They? There's no *they*. It's only him." He pointed at me.

The woman named Alice and I whipped our heads around at the same time. Will was nowhere to be seen. She threw me a puzzled look. For the daughter of a spy, however, a quick lie is child's play.

I shrugged. "Will must have slipped out into the alley. He told me once that high ceilings like this make him nervous and afraid to talk, as if he's in church. He's probably waiting out front for me right now," I finished, but without much conviction. The scoundrel owed me a full two hours, and I would get it from him or challenge him to a real duel.

"He's an odd one, isn't he?" Alice asked.

The man named Basset folded his arms and cocked his chin at me. "You said you came to find out about Sally. What's she done now?"

"She's missin'," Alice answered for me. "That's what. She hasn't been to work in two days."

He nodded, gave me another look of scrutiny and then headed toward the door that I guessed led into the main part of the house. "When she comes in, tell her I need to see her. You know how Lord Wotton always likes to have her at his beck and call. And I'll wager she'll be wantin' somethin' when she comes in. No matter what she has, she's always wantin' more."

He glanced at his image in a shiny copper pot that hung by the door and smoothed down his wavy, black locks. Then he left without saying good-bye.

"Aye," Alice said to the closed door, "I'll tell her, right after she helps me get ready for this dinner party."

She turned to the work table behind her and snatched up a pitcher. I cringed, thinking she was about to throw it. Instead, she poured some milk into a bowl and set it on the floor for the cat. Cringing didn't seem to occur to him. He rubbed against her legs and lapped up the milk.

Will or no Will, and blast him for being a scoundrel, I should at least be asking questions. That was what I came here to do.

"The last time Sally was here, did she say anything about running away?"

Alice put her hands on her hips and reared her head back. "Sally never talked to me any more than she had to, as if I wasn't good enough for her."

"I've never met the girl," I said with a grudging smile, "but I'm beginning to wonder what my cousin sees in her."

"I told you, a pretty face and a figure men go giddy for." She shook her head and made a scolding noise.

64

"Even old Lord Wotton got taken in by that trollop. Anyway, you know what I mean. You men are all alike."

I felt my face turn red. For a minute there, I had forgotten who I was. But I was saved by a loud knock on the door to the alley. It opened and the vigorous, dirt-streaked face of a young man appeared. He wore rough, workman's clothes and a cap that was pulled down low over his forehead. His face was vaguely familiar. He also half-hid himself behind the door.

"Hello, Alice, love. And how might you be this fine afternoon, my little sweetheart? Are you gettin' things ready for the dinner party?"

"Maybe I am. Maybe I'm not," she said warily.

"I'll tell my brothers to come 'round tomorrow to help you out. Basset will be hirin' more servants for his lordship, won't he?"

"Maybe he will. Maybe he won't." She had not taken her eyes off him.

"Is...uh...is Sally around?" he asked.

Without a word, she picked up an apple from the table and fired it at him. He was quick, though, and closed the door. The projectile bounced off the wood and rolled across the floor to bump against my shoe.

The man was undeterred. He opened the door once more and rushed up to her, taking both her hands in one of his and putting an arm around her waist. Even through the workman's jacket he wore, I could see that he had large arm and shoulder muscles.

65

"Now, Alice," he began in a cajoling tone. On his face was a smile about two sizes too big. "You know how I feel. You're the only woman for me. I was wonderin' about Sally purely for her mother's sake. Her mother's worried sick about her. And besides," he added with a sneer, "I'm not interested in that girl. She thinks she's too good for me."

In Alice's place, I would not have believed the oily, young man. He had all the sincerity of a cat that rubs up against your legs just before meal-time. (At least the tabby had seemed to thank her for the milk.) Alice thawed under his warm gaze.

And she was giving me a sidelong look.

"This here is Luke," Alice said to him. "Luke's come to…to visit me."

The woman could give writing lessons to Will. In my brief career as a male, no woman had yet used me to make someone else jealous. I just wished that this first someone else wasn't quite so...large.

He turned his false smile in my direction and dropped his jaw. I think he saw me for the first time. And he did not like what he saw. Dropping Alice's hands, he advanced toward me, pulling off his cap as he came. I didn't like what I saw either. Now I realized why he looked familiar. This dirty-faced suitor was my swordsman of the morning, Patrick, the man who had vowed to kill me.

His hand edged to a belt loop on his pants and rested on the handle of his sword.

Not to be outdone, I pulled my sword from its sheath and stood ready for battle.

"Oh, no!" Alice screamed. "Not in my kitchen."

But it was too late.

He drew his sword and took a step toward me. In place of the false smile he had given Alice was a dark scowl. "I'll teach you," he said between clenched teeth. "You won't come sniffin' 'round my woman again."

CHAPTER 4
A HEAD UPON A PIKE

I stared at him, dumbfounded. Had I heard right? Could it be that this man did not recognize me, someone he had tried to kill only a few hours earlier? I gathered my wits. "Never mind about Alice," I said to the man, hoping to forestall any bloodshed, especially mine. "Tell me about this... Rosemary. Who is she, and what has she to do with me?"

"Rosemary?" Alice's voice was shrill. "First Sally, and now another woman?" Now it was his turn to look confused. "Rosemary?" he echoed. Then his eyes shifted slowly from me toward Alice, but halted halfway between us. He froze in place. "Are you a ghost?" he whispered. "You weren't there before."

My fingers tightened on my sword, till I realized he was looking at the wall past my left shoulder. It was the oldest trick in the world. "You think I'll fall for that?" I asked, but he made no reply. Only when Alice pointed wordlessly at the wall did I turn my head and there stood Will, as calm as a locked gate.

Will gestured toward the kitchen's high ceiling. "Perhaps I descended from the heavens like some actor in a play."

My adversary lowered his sword. After all, Will was bigger than I.

"It's just funny I didn't see you before now," he said.

"Yes, isn't it?" Will agreed, pulling away from the wall and moving slowly in my direction. I put my sword back into its sheath, breathing a prayer I would not need it again today.

"You are a quick one, Will," Alice said admiringly. "I never saw you slip in, either. Will's looking for Sally, too," she said, with a meaningful glance at her suitor.

"Oh?" The muscles in the man's upper arm bulged like the bag end of a bellows. He narrowed his eyes again, and I instinctively held my breath. "You know Sally, then?" he asked softly. "When did you see her last?"

"The truth is," Will began, taking a black velvet cap from his pocket and setting it at a jaunty angle atop his head, "the truth is, I've never seen her last. I would imagine that only her shoemaker has had that pleasure."

The man screwed up his face in puzzlement. "Shoemaker? Pleasure? You talk nonsense."

Will reached my side and pulled me along to the door. When he opened it, and we stood safely on the threshold, he turned back to shake his head sadly in an exaggerated way, as if he were still onstage. "The greater nonsense is to talk at all, when such a pretty maid is waiting to be kissed."

My last glimpse of that kitchen showed Alice putting a floury hand on the man's chin and drawing his face to hers. He seemed surprised, but he did not resist. Will closed the door firmly, and we turned to leave.

A surprise of a different kind was waiting for us outside. I no sooner turned around than I felt and saw the point of a sword on the tip of my nose. My eyes crossed. In front of me, but blurred like an image through a fog, was the figure of a man. A large man. I think I stopped breathing.

"Sir," I heard Will say, "sheathe your sword or there will be the devil to pay."

"Ha! You don't frighten me," the large man said. He didn't even bother to glance in Will's direction. "I have a sword very close to your friend's throat. I think it's safe to say that I'm in charge here."

Out of the corner of my eye, I saw Will draw his sword and advance on the other fellow. Confusion filled the stranger's large, round eyes.

"You presume he is my friend," Will said. "Actually, I was about to steal his purse. But yours looks much heavier, sir. And your hands are otherwise occupied."

The sword departed from the neighborhood of my nose and began whipping the air in Will's vicinity, giving me time to pull my sword from its scabbard. My prayer had gone no higher than Alice's spider-strung kitchen ceiling.

We backed him against the bricks of Lord Wotton's home. With only a gesture, Will demanded the man's sword. I took it from his outstretched hand.

"And your purse," Will added.

I took the purse, also, but raised my eyebrow at Will.

"Who are you?" Will demanded.

"B-Brooke," the man mumbled. "Stephen Brooke."

Fat drops of sweat rolled down his cheeks. He had the kind of face I've always called pretty, even on a man: clear, rosy skin, thick, dark eyebrows over dark eyes, a short, straight nose and full lips. I could picture him on a stage, costumed, bewigged and rouged. Of course, his physique was much too big to play most women's roles, and his face was too fine to play most men's.

Will pulled the cap farther onto his forehead. "Why did you draw a sword on my friend here?"

"Your friend?" Brooke's eyes shifted to me. "I...uh... I'm looking for a girl."

Will suddenly stepped back and sheathed his sword. Stephen Brooke blinked and took his first deep breath in several minutes. Will folded his arms and smiled, a calculating smile, though I doubted that Brooke could see it under the shadow of the black cap.

"I must apologize, Mr. Brooke. Only a fool or a blind man would mistake my friend here for a girl. Which are you, sir?"

Will's flowery words did not make me withdraw my sword, however. Mine was the nose Brooke had tickled, and my weapon did not stray from his throat.

"No, of course not. Never mistake you," the man said to me, his full lips trembling. "I mean that I'm looking for a girl who works here. Sally Clopton. I, I thought you might...know her."

"Know her in what way?" Will's voice was teasing. "In the way that Adam knew Eve?"

Brooke flicked him an irritated glance but quickly brought his gaze back to my hand. "I thought you might know of her, what kind of woman she is or where she is."

71

"What kind of woman is Sally, Mr. Brooke?" Will gave me an encouraging nod, and I moved my hand forward a fraction of an inch. My sword hand.

"She...uh...she can't be trusted. You shouldn't trust her."

Will motioned for me to sheathe my sword, and I did. This fellow obviously had no useful information.

"We'll leave your sword somewhere in the next street or two, Mr. Brooke. I trust that we will not encounter it or you again."

We turned and began to walk away. Will did not have to tell me to walk slowly. From the silence behind us, I guessed Mr. Brooke did not move until we were out of sight. While I tried to breathe normally, Will examined the man's sword. When we reached a square filled with shops and shoppers, he removed his own sword and casually left it on the stoop of a building. Then he put Brooke's sword into his scabbard.

"The metal's much better than mine," he said when I raised an eyebrow. "What would you do?"

I did not say a word.

He resumed walking, and I rushed to catch up with him.

"Besides," he added under his breath, "when one steals a nobleman's purse, one would be wise to keep his sword as well. Don't you agree?"

"Stephen Brooke is a nobleman?"

Stephen Brooke, Lord Pettigrew. I recognized the name but had seen the face only from a distance before. "I just hope he didn't get a good look at me," he said and then grinned mischievously. "In my defense, though, I had no idea of Pettigrew's pedigree till after my petty larceny."

I rolled my eyes. "Aren't you afraid he'll want revenge?"

"More afraid that I may need to approach him for patronage someday, or that the troupe may. Plus, if he ever goes to the theater, he may see me perform. I don't need the notoriety."

"Is that why you wore that cap low over your eyes? No, wait." I stared at him. "You put the cap on while we were still in the kitchen. Why?"

"Discretion," he said with a broad grin, "is the better part of long life. Your kitchen combatant impressed me as hot-blooded. I didn't want him recognizing my face, either. Thought I'd limit his exposure to it. Maybe it worked, maybe it didn't," he added with a shrug.

"Speaking of the fellow, that was my second exposure to him today."

Will looked at me skeptically, and I told him briefly about the sword fight in the square.

"It's odd, though. He did not seem to recognize me the second time."

"Rosemary," he repeated, ignoring my last statement. "I take it the kitchen maid's name is not Rosemary, then?"

I shook my head. "Alice."

"Perhaps it was noisy in the square this morning," he said. "Could you have misunderstood him?"

"I don't think so."

"Still," he went on, "the word makes no obvious sense. Perhaps it's a symbol. Rosemary is an herb, you know. Apothecaries claim it's good for the memory."

I pounded my fist into my palm. "But the biggest mystery is why I ran into the blasted fellow again today, and clear across London?"

"Hmm." Will rubbed his chin. "Definitely a coincidence. I don't think I could get away with that in a play, unless there was a good reason for it. I'd say there's a reason for your seeing him again today, but you haven't figured it out yet."

"I hope I live long enough to figure it out."

"Another mystery," Will said, "is Sally's reputation."

"What do you mean?"

"Don't you think it's odd that so many men, men of very different backgrounds, have an interest in this girl?"

"Thomas said she was beautiful. Alice said so, too." I wasn't sure what Will was getting at, and I wondered if another man might. I needed to sound like a man. "Beautiful women," I began haltingly.

"Yes," Will said. "I think I know what you were about to say. Beautiful women make their own society."

I smiled and nodded, as if I had been about to say just that.

"But perhaps, in her spare time," Will went on, "perhaps Sally was also a prostitute." He spoke as casually as if he had called her a seamstress.

I felt myself blush and kicked at a pebble in the street. I didn't like what his remark implied about Thomas.

"Enough about Sally," I said abruptly. "Back at Lord Wotton's just now, where did you go when you left the kitchen? I told Alice you slipped out the back. She may have believed that, but I didn't."

"Let's find a place to sit and I'll tell you. No, I'll show you. As the immortal Chaucer said, 'Showing is better than telling.'"

"I don't recall any line like that in..."

"Perhaps I've improved on Chaucer's style. As I recall, his exact words were,

I want a man who'll do and not just tell.
Examples, not sermons, keep souls from hell."

"That still doesn't sound like..."

"You like to argue, don't you? Well," he broke off, frowning at something over my shoulder. "I wouldn't have thought we'd walked this far."

I looked around, surprised that we had reached the river. Usually, I can smell it long before I see it. The Thames is too far inland to carry much salt with it, but the tang of fish and the day's cast-off garbage has a bouquet not to be sniffed at. Dumping in the Thames is illegal, but people do it anyway, late at night when constables would likely be at home in their beds. In a boathouse below us, I could see the bow of a barge and craned my neck to get a better look. Just as I suspected, it was the Queen's. A painter was touching up the red petals in the large Tudor Rose, the emblem of her family. Something was written on the eaves just above the man's head, and I squinted to make out the words. Carpentry and Warehousing, the sign said, followed by some faded letters and then the single word, Street.

What street, I wondered idly? I had always prided myself on knowing the names of London's byways, but I had never considered these places tucked under the wharf to be authentic streets.

"Let's stop here for a while," I said, signaling a halt and leaning against a sawed-off timber. The sun glinted above the horizon, tingeing the river and everything around us with a golden aura.

"That Alice is quite dramatic." Will sat atop the next timber and stroked his chin. "I may give one of the female characters in my play some of her liveliness. You know, the little maid might do very well in the theater. Too bad women aren't allowed on the English stage. In Italy, by contrast..."

"Don't you ever tire of talking?"

He cocked his head as if he had never been asked that before. With his long, dark hair, golden earring and muscular build, he looked as if he might have just come out of one of these warehouses after a hard day's work.

"Forget Italy," I went on. "Tell me where you were ten minutes ago. You were not standing in that kitchen the whole time. I don't believe that for a minute. And you owe me for the time you were out of the room."

Instead of answering at once, he pulled a slim book from a jacket pocket.

"I took this from Lord Wotton's library, a most impressive room with almost as many sculptures as it has books, and with bookshelves nearly as high as the domed ceiling." He traced the title of the book with his finger as he read it aloud. *"His True Art of Defense* by Giacomo di Grassi."

"Is the book a clue to help us find Sally?" I asked with genuine naiveté.

"No," he said with a laugh. "It's a book I borrowed from his lordship. I was looking for something else, but this was all I had time to take."

"What?"

"Well, I was looking for a copy of Reginald Scot's *Discovery of Witchcraft,* but this will do in the meantime."

I leaped to my feet. "No, no. You misunderstand me. I meant, what were you thinking of, stealing a book from that house? Have you lost your mind?"

He seemed to be studying my anger, as if he might make use of it in one of his plays. He even grinned at me and twirled the golden hoop in his ear. "You'll have to decide that after you've known me awhile," he said. "For the moment, leaf through this book with me." He began flipping the pages. "It was published two years ago, but his lordship hasn't even trimmed all the ends yet."

He was right. Most of the ends were still folded crisply and still uncut. I had heard of the book, but Father refused to get me a copy. An unfeminine choice, he had said. I bent closer to the page and spoke before I thought.

"I wonder if di Grassi suggests how to perfect one's imbrocata."

"Here," Will said, patting the other half of his timber. I sat. "There you are. Now look at this with me. Why should books be held prisoner by only a few privileged people? Someday, when I've gleaned everything I can from this book, I'll return it to Lord Wotton. When I'm wealthy myself, I'll hire a boy, someone like you, perhaps," he added, running his eyes up and down my frame, "who will deliver a plain, paper-wrapped package to his lordship's door, with the simple message, 'Thank you for the loan. A friend.' If I feel very generous, I'll include a short poem, written especially for the occasion."

I could feel myself being swayed by his logic as I watched him slowly thumb the pages, like a gourmet savoring a treat. The book had an occasional drawing, I noticed. Will flipped back to the beginning for me, and I read the inscription. It was in Latin in a beautiful handwriting. "Charley," it read, "Amor magnus doctor est Sophie."

"Charley, Love is a great teacher Sophie," Will translated aloud as if for my benefit. "It's a quote from St. Augustine," he added, giving me a sidelong glance.

"I can read," I snapped and then sanity returned. I jumped to my feet again. "Look here. This isn't right.

Do you perform this sort of larceny often? Is this why you find out where the nobility live in London? More to the point, is this why you suggested going to Lord Wotton's in the first place? You intended to steal a book from his lordship all along, didn't you?"

I did not succeed in ruffling a single feather on that marvelous peacock. He merely stroked his chin and watched me rant.

"Everyone, including you," he finally said, "has more than one motive for doing anything. What's your motive in looking for Sally, for instance? Are you filled with concern for her or for Arthur or for their mother? Probably not. You want to help your cousin, you say. Even there, Luke, you may have hidden reasons, ones that would be hard to explain. Maybe it's as simple as wanting to impress me, so that I'll write a part for you in my play and then persuade Mr. Bright to hire you."

I smiled and shook my head. There was no way I could tell this man that his devilish good looks were the chief reason I'd suggested spending two hours together.

"How about yourself, Will? I doubt your heart's being tugged by the missing girl, either. Granted, you had to come along with me, but you were probably hoping something would happen that you could use. I bet you use every experience in your life in your writing." I finished on a high note of self-righteousness.

"I plead guilty!" he said with a wicked grin. "And if I'm going to learn anything else today, we'd better get started soon, before it gets much darker. By my calculation,

I owe you another fifty minutes. I'm sure you have a destination in mind." He stood, dropped the book into a pocket and stretched his arms.

I wasn't expecting this sudden turnaround, but he was right. I did have another destination in mind.

"We need to go to Sally's house in Southwark."

He did not disagree, though we had words about the method of getting there. He wanted to walk across London Bridge, but I wanted to hire a ferry for a penny. Will maintained that walking would actually be quicker now that the tide had come in. I peered over the side of the wall where we'd been sitting and counted a dozen boats at the ramp below us. Countless others were continually coming and going. At this time of day, there might be as many as a thousand small boats in the river, each one helmed by a man eager to earn a good tip for a fast trip. This heavy traffic would daunt even the helmsman of the Queen's barge. It was no wonder Her Majesty preferred to sail late in the evening. Besides, I didn't have a penny.

"Let's walk, then," I said. "I can compromise as well as the next man."

Will's broad shoulders helped cut a swath for us in the late-afternoon traffic. The crowd swelled here and ebbed there, but he kept a steady pace. On we slogged across the bridge through a sea of humanity, past the clamorous shopkeepers, the yelping dogs, the rude wagon drivers with their gassy, slow-moving horses, and the smells of warm bread and hot sausages being sold on either side of us. Suddenly, I realized I was starving. The last food between my lips was a hasty breakfast with Thomas. About halfway across the bridge, I halted in front of a vendor's booth and pulled out my pockets to show Will they were empty.

"Lend me the money for a sausage," I said, "and I'll tell you the story of my relative who lost his head."

He raised his dark eyebrows. "Losing your head may be a Culpeper family trait."

"Come on," I wheedled. "The story says much about human nature, and it's relevant to this very bridge. Besides, if you buy a sausage for yourself, you'll have something to occupy your hands when we pass the bookstalls."

We were soon on our way again. I don't usually talk with food in my mouth, but bridge traffic encourages yelling and shoving, not good manners.

"It happened in 1541," I began, "when King Henry was married to...wait, I always forget this. Let's see, how does the little song go...

Divorced, beheaded, died,

Divorced, beheaded, survived.

First, of course, there was Catherine of Aragon whom he divorced. Then Anne Boleyn whom he beheaded in 1536, I believe. Next, Jane Seymour who died soon after childbirth. Then came Anne of Cleves in 1540 whose title was removed, instead of her head, the following year. Very soon afterward, he married Katherine Howard. And so, it was this Katherine who was married to King Henry in 1541." I stopped, pleased at my memory.

Just then we had to suspend conversation to maneuver around a large, loud hurdy-gurdy. The two men playing the instrument were singing a French ballad with—strange as it seems—Italian accents. Several other bridge-crossers had stopped with us as well. The performers' striking features and Mediterranean coloring added high drama to the song about a faithless lover. When they finished, a few of us clapped, and Will threw Stephen Brooke's purse into a brass pot at their feet. The older singer, who also supplied the hand-cranking, nodded and smiled.

"Grazie!" he called out and began another tune.

Will smiled back and made a graceful half-bow as he turned to leave. We resumed our walk toward the Southwark side of the bridge.

"Finish your little story," he said, waving his fingers like a king to his jester.

If there had been a break in the crowd, I would cheerfully have flung him from the bridge. Instead, I did exactly as he said. Why was I so bent on pleasing this man?

"Queen Katherine," I began, "was very immature when she married King Henry. She was eighteen, I think, with some modern ideas about marriage. In her leisure time, she shared her bed with two of her husband's hunting companions. On his own, the King probably never would have discovered her unfaithfulness, but some of his meddlesome ministers insisted on telling him. One of the guilty men was Francis Dereham, whom Katharine knew before becoming queen, and the other was my great-uncle, the gallant and handsome Thomas Culpeper. Uncle Thomas denied

82

the charge, of course, to save the Queen's honor, but too many people testified against him. He couldn't even save his own head, which, once they cut it off, was displayed on a pike atop this very bridge."

A rag-tag family with four rowdy, dirty children approached. Edging to the side of the bridge to let them pass, I saw Will do the same, and my arm pressed against a thick, wooden support. I stroked the weathered grain, and wondered how many other Londoners might have touched this very beam over the years, and a new thought struck me. Had my great-uncle Thomas ever walked across this strong, wide bridge? Had he stopped, perhaps, in this very spot? I roused myself from my reverie, afraid of losing Will's interest. He had been quiet for a full minute, at the least.

"The Queen's other lover," I went on, "was drawn and quartered, but Thomas was a special friend of the king's, so he was only beheaded. In those days, you may know, the skulls of traitors were left atop the bridge as a kind of *memento mori* to the rest of the citizenry, a way of saying, 'Remember. You, too, must die.' It was before my time, but Father said my great-uncle's head stayed up there for eight or nine years, picked clean till only the skull was left."

I glanced to the side to check Will's reaction. He had come to a standstill and was studying something high above us. I stopped beside him, following his gaze upward. Nothing at all hung on the jagged pikes today, nothing but a piece of moon that looked as if it had been snagged, mid-sky. We looked away from the pikes at the same time, and our eyes locked. I had meant to entertain, to fill a quarter-hour, to make him remember my narrative skills and create a role just for me. I had not meant to make him sad.

"You won't find this observation in a book," he said softly, "or in your family history, but I think Katherine Howard never intended to keep her marriage vows." He raised his eyes back to the pikes high overhead. "Some women are like that. Born to lie, my friend, to any man with whom they lie."

Someone jostled me. Traffic was heavier now, and I reached out to steady myself. His wrist was the thing my fingers clutched at, and he shook his head as if I'd roused him from sleep. The dark eyes lost their frown. He clapped me on the shoulder, man to man, and laughed.

"You make me forget that you're just a boy, Luke. Come along."

I ran to catch up with him, vaguely aware that I had just witnessed an important scene, though uncertain how it fit into the whole drama. But I had no time to ponder. The winnings from my wager, one-hundred-twenty tiny pieces of time, were disappearing fast.

As our feet touched the marshy land of Southwark, the bells of St. Savior's church rang out. Six times the mellow gonging wrapped around us, followed by the familiar, comforting melody of the old St. Wilfred Evening Song.

"That's it!" I said, stopping to stare up at the old bell tower. The sky behind it was streaked with the last rays

84

of the sunset, but there was still enough daylight to find our way. I could see the small rectory beside the church.

"That's what?" Will asked.

"The church."

"Why, so it is," he said dryly. "How astute of you to notice."

"No, you don't understand what I mean. If anyone in this town would know where the Clopton family lived, it would be the rector, don't you think?"

He looked past me at the church. "You're probably right, but my time would be up before we reached Sally's house. Even St. Wilfred agrees with me." He pointed to the bell tower.

I stared at him, but not in disappointment. A good spy always masks her feelings.

"I understand," I said. "Time's money, to quote the playwright himself. You're a good sport, Will. See you around."

I turned and headed toward the rectory. It was almost dark. This quest would not be as much fun alone, but I could not stop now.

CHAPTER 5
NEITHER RHYME NOR REASON

I had gotten to the front door and was lifting my hand to knock when I heard a noise behind me. Grabbing at my sword, I wheeled around. The man approaching me raised his hands to show he meant no harm. A light from within the house glinted off his earring.

"I decided I could not let you out-gentleman me," he said.

"No danger in that." I turned back, breathed a prayer of thanks and rapped on the door.

A small, elderly woman, shiny-faced, trusting, opened it at once. "May I help you?"

Will's sudden defection and re-enlistment had caught me unprepared. "Uh, we...we're friends of Sally Clopton," I began weakly.

The woman's hand went to her cheek. Her blue eyes watered. "Oh, my! My husband only just left to tell her family. How did you find out so soon?"

"Uh, that is..."

Will stepped to the door. "We ran into him on the way and wondered how we might help."

"That's very kind. I'm sure her parents will be grateful. I suppose you could go out to keep watch beside her body. My husband hated to leave her out there, but at the same time, he needed to tell her parents and the constable."

"That's the least we can do," he went on. "Where can we find .her body?"

She pointed past us. "Over there, through the iron gate. He left it open."

We said good-bye and moved off into the gathering darkness. The old woman called out as an afterthought.

"She's in the northern part of the cemetery, in the Single Woman's Graveyard. Her family won't like that at all. The poor girl did away with herself, my husband says. He found her hangin' by the neck."

"Well, then," Will said softly, casting his dark eyes down at me. "I guess we'll be looking for a tall tree, won't we?"

When we reached the gate, darkness had erased all trace of daylight. Only a quarter-moon high above us lit our way, and I began to have second thoughts about entering a cemetery. This particular graveyard was immense. The horizon was dotted with headstones, like slats on a garden fence.

"This is no longer just an afternoon's lark, you know."

Will's voice startled me. There was no fear in his eyes, only amusement.

"What do you mean?"

"Now there's a corpse. Do you still want to see this through to the end?"

I held his gaze. Smugness in a man brings out the worst in me.

"Your two hours are up. I can find her body by myself."

He pushed against the gate and walked through without glancing at me. "No, I can't let you do that. Your big Bernard of a cousin would break me in half for abandoning you in a graveyard. Besides, I've never seen a body hanging from a tree, have you?"

"That's because you're not a native Londoner," I replied, running to keep pace with his longer legs. "We get used to dodging them." I tripped over a low grave marker, and he steadied me with his hand.

"Yes. I can see how agile you've become. You know, a man could make a fortune selling torch lights in a place like this. There's a piece of a moon and a few stars. They might help."

"They would help if we were sailors," I said, "but I think we'll have to navigate by our own lights, so to speak. Remember that the old woman told us Sally's body is in the north end of the graveyard. We just have to go in that direction." I pointed toward our right and started off again.

"How do you know that's north?"

"By the way the graves are laid out. In Christian cemeteries, bodies are buried facing the east, to be ready for the Resurrection." I shrugged as if anyone should have known that.

"There's more to you than meets the eye, young Luke."

I gave him a sidelong glance. "If you mean that I'm more intelligent than I look, it works to my advantage. What is that?" I pointed to a shadow far ahead. "Does that look like a tree?"

"Very like a tree. Watch out for the..."

I tripped over another low headstone, stopped to slap the mud off my leggings and began talking to cover my embarrassment. "The rector's wife called the place where we'll find Sally's body the Single Woman's Graveyard. Do you know why?"

"No." He grinned and affected a lower-class, country accent. "I'm a newcomer to these parts, remember?"

"Then I'll entertain you as we walk. Years ago, that particular graveyard was set aside just for prostitutes. There were brothels here."

"Seems odd," he said, "to have brothels on ground that once was holy, doesn't it?"

"What seems odd to me," I countered, "is what the rector's wife told us. If Sally killed herself, why'd she do it there? I mean, it's a place where prostitutes were buried." As we walked, I gestured to the graves all around us. "You wondered if Sally might be a prostitute, but even if she was, no girl in her right mind would go to that section of the cemetery to commit suicide. That would be like announcing it to the world."

"Unlike you," he said quickly, "I don't pretend to know with certainty what goes on in a girl's mind."

I opened my mouth to argue but realized I would only make things worse.

As Will and I made our way through the cemetery, the sliver of moon showed itself, and I saw for the first time how much these headstones and footstones resembled beds. Off to our left, a child's grave carried the likeness further: the headstone had a curving base, like a tiny cradle. As if, it seemed to me, the parents could not bear to think of their child as dead, but only as...

"There she is." Will's voice startled me, and I jumped.

It was a girl's body, all right. Her white dress swirled in the breeze.

I had lied to Will. I was not accustomed to such a sight, nor was I prepared for it.

"Do you still want to finish this?" Will asked softly, without waiting for an answer.

He reached the tree before I did and studied the body closely. I stood rigidly a few feet away.

"It's Sally," he said, "but her own mother might not know her."

She was hanging by the neck, just as the old woman had said. I would have to rely on Thomas's word that Sally had been a beautiful girl. Now, the skin on her swollen face was the same dull gray as the headstones that ringed the tree. Her long black hair was tangled and matted. Her eyes were open but vacant.

I stepped forward a little, and the skin on my cheeks tightened. Sally's face and neck and arms were covered with countless cuts and gashes, each one encrusted with red-black blood.

"Rat bites, I'd guess," Will said. He pinched the blue-white skin of Sally's wrist. "Her body must have been kept somewhere, hard to tell for how long. Then she was brought here when no one else was around."

I jerked my head toward him. "You don't think it was suicide? But the old woman said..."

"The murderer wants it to look like suicide, but he did at least four things wrong. Look here. Let's start at the top. What do you see on her neck?"

"A rope."

"Good," he said, rolling his eyes. "But look at that rope carefully. In order to make such a tight knot around the tree limb, she must have stood on a ladder or some other support. But where's the ladder? And for the second clue, look at her throat, just below the rope. See those bruises? I think someone strangled her first and then hanged her to make it look like a suicide. The third thing is her shoes. Check the soles."

I did and saw at once what he meant. The bottoms of her shoes were clean. Anyone walking in this cemetery in the last few days would have had muddy shoes. As I knelt, the wind rustled around us. Under Sally's apron, just at her waist, a flash of color fluttered against the white skirt. Without thinking, I stood on tiptoe and tugged on the colored object. It must have been tied loosely, and it fell into my hand, a woman's drawstring bag. The fabric felt like rich damask.

Just as my fingers closed over it, Will grabbed my wrist.

"It was an accident," I hissed.

He put a finger to his lips and looked in the direction we had come. In the distance, a torch bobbed toward us. Voices floated on the breeze.

Will turned and began to move in the opposite direction, away from the torch, dragging me along with him. Why we weren't impaled on headstones or tripped senseless by footstones, I'll never know.

Long minutes later, we found a road and circled back. The bell tower of St. Savior's loomed ahead, black against the sky. I didn't have the breath to speak until we were on the bridge again. We had little company.

"Why did we run?" I finally asked. "That was probably Sally's family."

"And the rector," he added. "And probably a constable. I don't know about you, but I keep track of the lies I tell, and I couldn't think of a way to explain our presence. I'd told the rector's wife that we had seen her husband. What could we tell him? That we'd just happened to wander by and ran into this dead body? Sorry, but I can't always fashion fiction on such short notice."

"In that case," I said softly, "perhaps a writing career doesn't suit you."

"Why, you..."

He halted. So did I. Anger filled his eyes, until he saw my smile. His mouth curved upward as if mimicking me. The distance between us grew taut, like the line from a ship to its anchor.

"You...you can let go of my wrist," I said.

He did, and we resumed walking. There were no vendors now, and only a few torches blazed from the bridge railings. A fog shrouded everything more than ten feet away. From the London side, I heard a church bell toll seven times. The day was nearly over. The two hours' time I'd won from Will had flown by. For some reason, out of courtesy, a sense of honor, a taste for my wit, he had given me more than two hours. Would I ever see him again? My mind raced feverishly.

"What...what was that fourth clue?"

"Hmm?" His eyes seemed to be searching for something far ahead of us, perhaps the lights of London.

"You said there were four clues that showed Sally was murdered. You only told me about three of them: the rope on the tree limb, the bruises on her throat and the soles of her shoes. What was the fourth one?"

"Oh, that." He gestured to the wood planks at our feet. "There were wagon wheel ruts under the tree. I guessed that whoever murdered her had brought her body to the cemetery in the wagon that left those ruts."

I nodded.

"You said that your cousin Thomas cared for Sally," he went on. "Will you tell him about this?"

I nodded again and bit my lip.

"Are you certain," he asked, "absolutely certain, that Thomas cared for her?"

"Of course. Why would you ask that?"

In the semi-darkness, I tried to read his face.

He shrugged. "I was just thinking of everyone who might have had a motive to murder her. Sometimes passion is ample provocation."

I halted in the middle of the bridge.

93

"Are you accusing Thomas of murdering Sally?" My hand flew to my sword. "Because if you are..."

A slow grin spread over his roguish face. "I was just thinking aloud, Luke. I didn't accuse your cousin of anything, not even love. How old are you?"

"F-fifteen. Why?"

"If you want to live to be sixteen, take some advice. Learn the difference between accusation and supposition. If I wanted to suggest that I suspect Thomas, I know the language to do it in. Come on, Luke." He narrowed his eyes and angled his head toward the London side of the bridge. "You seem like a mature young man. Act like one. Take your hand off your sword. I'll walk home with you, and you can listen to the names of the people I do suspect."

I fell into step beside him but told myself that I would not speak for at least a quarter of an hour, not until a church bell chimed again. I'd show him who could be mature!

"I don't suggest," he began, "that you and I should look for Sally's murderer. That's a job for the constable. But the cast of characters is intriguing, isn't it?"

I did not even nod my head but only tried to keep up with his longer stride.

"Almost like seeing a performance of a play, I think. In fact, I'll present the cast to you as if you were watching this on a stage. As Chaucer said, showing's infinitely better than telling. Do you have any objection?"

I did not move my head an inch.

94

"Good," he said and took a deep breath. "First, there's the victim, a young girl named Sally. You, of course, as the spectator of the play, would not know that Sally was once a beautiful girl. You did not meet her until she was quite dead, but several people onstage, rather like a Greek chorus, told you how stunning she was. Your cousin Thomas appreciated Sally's beauty, or so you led Alice to believe. Alice herself spoke bitterly of Sally's good looks. And then there's buxom Ellen. By the way, have you wondered whose blood Ellen may have used to write that note to Thomas?"

That question almost made me jerk my head toward him, but I folded my arms and concentrated on keeping up with his pace. He seemed not to notice, but went on with his cast of characters.

"The young man in Lord Wotton's kitchen—Patrick, was it?—He may have been under Sally's spell. He seemed jealous when he learned I knew the girl, too. For the moment, we will not even consider your initial run-in with him this morning. Mr. Brooke, our unfortunate swordsman, was also enamored of Sally's physical charms. And who knows? There may be dozens more in this city who knew the girl and thought her beautiful. But anyone writing this play would have to consider the question: Is beauty sufficient motive for murder?" He paused as if waiting for my response, but I bit my tongue. In the distance, a church bell tolled. "I've always thought," he went on, "that temperament was more important than motive. Ten people may have a motive to murder someone, but only one of them may possess the temperament to carry out the crime. So, what do you think? Of the cast members I've presented so far, who seems likeliest to play the role of murderer?"

I hesitated, five seconds, ten, fifteen. In the afternoon performance of *The Mighty Myconides,* I had seen Will employ the dramatic pause very effectively.

"I think you've omitted certain suspects and motives, because you weren't privy to them."

"Indeed?" His eyebrows shot up. "Such as?"

"At the theater this morning, Gilbert Dereham muttered something strange, but I don't think anyone else heard. He called Thomas a pirate for stealing a beautiful woman from a man who'd seen her first."

"Hmm. I would not have thought Gilbert was Sally's type."

"Evidently, he thought so. And he does not like being corrected any more than you do. I merely pointed out to him that he had misused a certain Greek phrase, and you'd have thought I maligned his manhood."

"Interesting," Will said, "but I disagree with you. I never object to being corrected. Besides, you may have more in common with Dereham than I. The Dereham who committed adultery with Queen Katherine may have been his ancestor."

I shuddered. "I have nothing in common with that mountebank. At any rate, when you slipped out of Lord Wotton's kitchen, Basset, a servant, complained that Sally was always wanting something but never obeying him. I learned that Patrick may have been more than just charmed by Sally. She made him angry, by acting as if she were too good for him. Patrick has a brother who looks very much like him, the one who tried to kill Thomas. If they weren't so bent on homicide, they could take the roles of twins in that play you're writing, the one you called *The Comedy of Syracuse.*"

"The Comedy of Errors," he said with a grimace. "So you think you have found my *Dromio Erotes* and *Dromio Sereptus.* Perhaps you would like to write the play, as well?"

"Oh, I'm flattered that you think I could write it as well as you." I spoke quickly, incredulous that he had set me up for such a play on words, but his mind seemed to be somewhere else. He pulled at his mustache and squinted into the fog.

"Hmm," he said after a moment. "Flattered, you say. Young Sally was accustomed to flattery. Her connection to so many men intrigues me. Let me see that handbag of hers."

I pulled the bag from my pocket and tossed it to him.

He fought with the drawstrings for a moment and then threw it back to me.

"How do women operate these things?"

"Here, I watched Ellen open hers this afternoon," I said, catching myself just in time. "She pulled these strings." I flung it back to him.

He slipped his fingers into the bag and withdrew two items: a piece of paper the size of a place card, and a folded sheet of paper. Moving to a torch fixed to the railing, he opened the sheet of paper and spread it against the palm of his left hand.

"Peculiar style of language," he mumbled. "I detect neither rhyme nor reason. Holding it closer to the light, he began to read aloud, while I peered over his shoulder.

24
The Bazile never slumbers. Very soon the creature
Will sleep with the dead. The hope of the future will
Shoot forth from amidst the offal. Mark the Eve

At that moment, a cold rain started to fall, misting onto the paper. Wordlessly, Will dropped the note back into the bag and stashed the smaller card in a pocket of his vest. Had it not been raining, I would have demanded to see the card. When he offered Sally's bag to me, I slipped it inside my tunic and pulled my collar closer. We stepped from the shelter of the bridge onto London soil. The sliver of moon was gone, and it was quite dark, except for a sprinkle of light from an occasional window. I led him in the direction of my home, hoping that he would follow. He had promised to walk me home, but I already had been too lucky.

The rain slackened a bit just as we crossed a street ahead of a carriage. The horse's hooves made soft, sucking sounds in the mud. With a pang, I saw that we had reached the block where I lived. "This is home," I mumbled.

I had taken us to the door at the rear. There was room for both of us under the eave. Through the window, I saw

Cook moving around in the kitchen. Will took in the immensity of my home and its opulence without seeming to notice a thing. He and I have the same gift; perhaps that's why I recognize it in him. If he does not succeed as a writer (and if I did not like him so much), I could recommend him to Father for the spy business.

"Thanks for the two hours," I said. "You did more than our wager called for."

He grinned and stepped out from the eave. "Come back to the theater, Luke. Now I can recommend you to John Bright. I have seen you act."

With a wave, he set off down the alley. I watched him disappear into the dark night and puzzled over his remark. Except for my audition, when had he seen me act? The moment Will disappeared into the dark, rainy night, I slipped into the kitchen and ran to warm myself in front of the fire. The smell of stewed meat and onions filled the air, and I thought I would pass out from hunger. Asking for food, though, meant listening to Cook complain. She stood at the counter, with her back to me, pounding a loaf of sugar, and I was grateful for the noise of the mallet. Slowly, quietly, I tiptoed toward the door.

"Humph!" she snorted and turned around. "Don't think you can sneak past me, young miss. I saw you when you was standin' out in the rain."

She held the mallet chest-high, the way a smaller woman might point a finger. Cook had never been a small woman. Since I was a child, she had been tall and round and bewildered by me. I took the mallet from her and kissed the frown on her rough, red cheek. She clicked her tongue against her teeth and ran her eyes over me, as if I were a goose at market, and a skinny, unsatisfactory goose, at that.

"Why're you so bent on lookin' like a boy?" she asked.

"Life is very complicated, Cook." I gave an exaggerated sigh. "It's as hard to make a properly-brought-up young woman as it is to make your stuffed, roast goose for Christmas dinner." The daughter of a spymaster learns early how not to answer a question. I put the mallet back into her hand. "Has Thomas come by tonight?" I asked.

"I've not seen Thomas since this mornin' when you two left here together, both of you wearin' men's garments," she added with a scowl.

"May I have a bowl of sugar or is there anything else to eat?"

There was, in fact, mutton stew, but I had to pay for it. Her sermon on proper behavior lasted five minutes. And I listened to the first thirty seconds.

When I could stand no more, of the stew or the sermon, I said a demure "Thank you, Cook," and pushed my chair back from the table. She flung one last question as I reached the door to the hall.

"Who was that man just now, the one standin' next to you in the rain?"

I smiled, shook my head and pointed to my bulging cheeks. Any other young woman with a mouth full of mutton might have replied, but not the ladylike Lucinda Culpeper.

Less than half an hour later, I had hidden Sally's handbag under my pillow and bathed and dressed for bed. Now I looked nothing like a boy. I stood before a pier-glass in my bedroom and combed out my long, wet hair. A knock at the door made me jump.

"Who is it?" I called out. I had heard no one walking down the hall.

"Your father."

I leaped to open the door.

He stood there, motionless. As always, his appearance was neat and perfectly composed, from his short, gray hair to his shining, black boots. Behind their spectacles, his gray eyes took in everything about me without blinking. Unbidden, the image came to my mind of the view from that third-floor room into Father's study below. Many was the time I had watched him interrogate his agents. Most of them held up to his scrutiny. I gripped the edge of the door and smiled.

"Good evening, Father."

"I was just passing by," he said, "and realized I have not seen you for several days, Lucinda. How are you?"

"I'm fine, Father, perfectly fine."

"The staff tells me that you have kept to yourself lately. Where do you spend your time? Shall I hire a companion for you?"

"No, Father. There's no need. I, I've been in the attic much of the time," I said, fumbling with my hairbrush. "Reading...sewing. I've felt like being alone, I suppose."

"You suppose? Is there...anything you need to tell me, Lucinda? Is anything wrong?"

"Nothing is wrong, Father." I smiled sweetly, but behind the smile the mind of a spy's daughter machinated. He had once told an agent that distraction is the best method of manipulation, yet every distraction must serve some purpose, he had added. What was my purpose now? I recalled the one suspect in Sally's murder whom I had not yet met.

"In fact, Father, I ventured out for awhile today, and I saw someone, from a distance, that is. I didn't even know he existed. A very interesting-looking man. What do you know about Lord Charles Wotton?"

"Indeed? Is he back in London, then?"

"He must be, mustn't he?" I laughed nervously.

Father's eyes roved over my face. "The man seems much too old to spark your romantic interest, Lucinda. He's very wealthy, though. Lord Wotton is a widower. Did you know that?" He pursed his lips thoughtfully while I tried to conceal my confusion. How did Father get the notion that Lord Wotton had sparked my romantic interest? "Actually, now that I think about it," Father went on, "you would probably enjoy the man's company. He has a very large library, so I hear."

After today, Lord Wotton's library was smaller by one book, but I chose not to share that tidbit with my overly concerned father. A good spy would have gotten more information about Lord Wotton, but most spies don't have to deal with matrimonially-minded fathers.

Admonishing me to extinguish my light and go to sleep, Father said goodnight and closed the door. I was turning away, running the brush through my hair once more, when I heard a familiar footstep on the hall and then a familiar voice.

"Uncle Edward," Thomas called out. "May I see you, sir?"

"Of course," Father said. "Do you bring news?"

"Yes, sir."

"Let's go to my study."

Their footsteps faded away. In moments, I had changed into clean leggings, a fresh shirt and doublet, and was thrusting my hair under a cap. (Thank goodness, I had taken more than one set of clothing from Father's servant.) I glanced at my sword. Should I take it, I wondered, and then snatched it up. How many times today had I already needed this marvelous weapon? Better safe than sorry. After all, if I planned to follow Thomas home and tell the poor fellow about Sally, then I would need to be prepared for anything.

Stealthily, I tiptoed down the hall and up the rear stairs to the third floor. Cook's quarters were at the other end, but the second room on the right was the one I wanted. Quietly, I opened the door and crept to the far corner. I knew my way in the dark. As always, the frayed piece of carpet pulled easily from the floor. As always, I was able to look down into Father's study. He sat at his desk. Thomas sat in a chair near the fire, holding his cap in his hands and turning it over and over as he spoke.

103

"The truth is, sir, I failed."

"Tsk, tsk," Father said. "It's too early to speak of failure. The girl is dead, but you could not have prevented that."

"I failed to get any information from her, sir."

"We were never certain that she had information, Thomas. Your whole operation was based purely on the possibility that she might be delivering messages to Marshalsea Prison."

"Yes, sir, but something happened this morning, something that may prove..."

He hesitated.

"Prove what?" Father leaned forward.

"On the way to meet Sally, sir, two men stopped me. It was in a public square, but still they drew swords and tried their best to kill me. I had to draw blood to end it, sir, but not before one of them said the word." His voice became a whisper. "The word rosemary."

I dropped the piece of carpet and put my hand to my mouth. Thomas was a better actor than I thought. Slowly I pulled the carpet back again. Father was making notes, and Thomas continued to turn his hat over in his hands. "There's that word again." Father shook his head. "What can be the meaning? It's turned up in official dispatches, it's been overheard by agents from Cripplegate to the Tower, yet we have no hard information about it, only the suspicion that it portends imminent crisis. It's like something in the wind, something we can smell but cannot see."

I knew that my father was capable of deception. Anyone in the spy ministry has to be. As to persuading suspects, I had never seen him apply torture to anyone, but I had often wondered if he engaged in any tortures at the Tower, any *scraping of the soul*, as I had overheard one of his visitors remark. Most everyone in London knew what went on at the Tower, and some tortures were even public events. But to discover that Thomas, my Thomas, was capable of misleading me, *me* of all people, my mind reeled with the shock. His statement that he cared for Sally was a lie.

"You got away from both men, you say?" Father asked.

"Yes, sir. One of them won't be using a sword anytime soon."

"Well done, Thomas." Father reached out to grip Thomas's shoulder.

They made a striking tableau, Thomas's big body dwarfing my father's small, slim frame. I wondered, and not for the first time, if Father wished I had been a son.

Father sat back in his chair and tapped his chin thoughtfully. "The theaters are hotbeds of revolutionary thought. This is exactly why we place agents in the actors' troupes, Thomas. We stop a lot of trouble before it starts."

Of course, I thought. *That explains why I saw Christopher Marlowe here once, in the same chair Thomas was sitting in now.* Now Marlowe's visit made sense, but I was not prepared for the next revelation. "In fact," Father went on, "I recall when you infiltrated that very troupe last year, you found no evidence of political interest, did you?"

"No, sir," Thomas said. "None whatsoever." Their voices lowered, and I heard only bits and phrases after that: an address on Seething Lane; the name of Thomas Walsingham, Sir Francis's cousin; mention of Henry Rendle's work. In truth, I hardly listened. Thomas had joined the acting troupe, not to act, but to spy. Was there even now a spy in that troupe? In the near future, would someone be reporting the actions of a Luke Culpeper to my father?

As noiselessly as possible, I laid the carpet back in place and stood up. I had heard enough. Besides, if I planned to meet Thomas on his way home, I'd be wise to sneak out of the house before Father left his study.

Ten minutes later, I was standing in the shadow of a doorway just down the street, still plotting the way that I would reveal myself to my dear cousin. The possibilities were endless. Should I leap out and grab him around the neck? Should I trip him with my sword as he sauntered past? Someone approached, whistling low. Was it a tune or a signal? I recognized the tune and smiled smugly. It was one of Thomas's favorites. He whistled it often, especially when he was completely relaxed.

He was coming closer, closer. I made a fist and held my breath.

"Mmph! Hey!" Thomas cried out, and then he was silent.

I peered around the doorway. Two dark figures stood less than ten feet away, both very intent on their work. One pinned Thomas's arms from behind, while the other one methodically slammed his fist into Thomas's face and body.

I leaped out of my hiding place, my sword at the ready. I had never drawn so much as a thimbleful of blood before, but now I was prepared to litter the street with these villains, eager to cut them into pieces.

The one I reached first was pummeling Thomas's face. I plunged my sword into his upper arm just as he drew it back to strike again. The man yelled and slumped to the street, and I heard the metallic clink of his scabbard as it hit the cobblestones. Now I turned my attention to his companion, the one who had been occupied with holding Thomas. He dropped my cousin at once and put his right hand to his sword hilt. I achieved striking distance before the sword was halfway out.

"You!" he said, and I saw at once that it was Jack, the man from the morning's sword fight. A stained bandage swathed his lower left arm, so I gave him a matching wound on his right. He stumbled backward, falling over the body of his brother, who groaned and pushed him away.

"Thomas," I shouted. "Get up." Jack and Patrick were only wounded, so I could not afford to take my eyes from them for long. When Thomas did not answer, I flicked a glance at him. He was struggling to his feet, withdrawing his sword, but I did not think he could see well enough to fence. Both eyes were swollen almost shut.

"You! Jack," I yelled, "throw your sword against the wall." When he hesitated, I did not. My sword tore into his skin again, this time in his upper leg. "Now, do what I said." His weapon made a very satisfying *clank-clank* as it bounced off the bricks.

"Now your brother's," I said, and he leaned over to remove his brother's sword. In seconds, both weapons lay on the street several yards away. I kept my eyes on both men and backed away to the wall. One sword, I slipped into my scabbard; the other, I held in my left hand.

"Thomas," I said, sparing him a quick look. He was standing more steadily than before, but I still did not know if he could see. Perhaps no one else could tell, either. "Don't you want to ask these villains the meaning of the word *rosemary*?"

He nodded.

"Bring your sword here," I directed. "And here's an extra."

He walked toward the sound of my voice, his hand outstretched. When he was close enough, I put the grip of the sword into his hand, aiming the tip at the two men who cowered in front of us.

"There," I went on. "Now we can do some real interrogating." Thomas did not speak, so I assumed he could not. Of the four of us, I was the only non-casualty so far, but my bluster was wearing thin. "What does it mean, Patrick?" I asked again, standing as close as I dared, holding a sword in each hand. "You told me you would kill me. And you said that it was all because of *rosemary*."

When neither man replied, I added, "I already know it is not a woman, so come on. Out with it."

Beside me, I heard Thomas's ragged breathing. *Please, God,* I begged, *don't let him collapse. Not yet.*

Jack moaned and tried to sit up straight. He stared at his arms. Both were bleeding heavily now. Patrick pressed his left hand against the wound in his leg.

"It means," Jack began, but Patrick threw out his left hand and caught Jack on the mouth.

"Unh!" Jack cried out. He fell back to the street, unable to stop himself with his arms.

"Tell him, and he'll kill us both," Patrick said between clenched teeth.

"Luke," Thomas said, though it sounded more like "Ook."

I glanced his way. He lifted a sword and pointed off in the distance. A fog was settling in, but I saw what he meant. Several figures were headed our way. In the dark I couldn't tell who they were. I glared at Patrick.

"Till next time, laddie," I said. "Come on, Thomas."

I kept one eye on the wounded brothers and the other on Thomas. Quietly, the two of us backed away until we reached the next corner. There, we entered the fog ourselves.

Half an hour later, perhaps longer, we wound our way to the rear of my family's home. For the second time that night, I entered the kitchen. This time I used a key, and I pulled the latch behind us. A quarter of an hour earlier, Thomas and I had jettisoned the two extra swords. Tomorrow morning, some citizen was going to be very surprised when he opened his front door, and those gleaming weapons clattered into his foyer.

"In here," I whispered. The only other sound was Thomas's labored breathing. So far he had said nothing but my name, that one time.

I led him to the pantry and felt around for the stack of table linens. Cook was an organized woman who took pride in keeping things in their place.

"You can sleep here," I said, spreading the linens on the empty space in the middle of the pantry, and he sank onto the floor. My huge cousin looked pitifully small lying there on the white tablecloths. His face was painful to look at, and I winced to imagine how he must feel. It was not quite pitch black in the house. The rain had stopped, and the same sliver of moon that Will and I had seen in the graveyard sent a faint light through the kitchen window and into the pantry. "I'll see you in the morning," I said and turned to leave.

"Lucy." He reached out and clutched my hand. "Thank you."

I nodded, wishing that I were the kind of person who could leave certain things unsaid. But I am who I am. "It's a good thing those two men came along when they did. Otherwise," I paused dramatically, "I was ready to kill you myself."

"What?" He raised his head. In the shadows, his face was a mass of purple shadows. I sat on a sack of potatoes.

"Thomas, you lied to me. You weren't in love with Sally. You were acting on orders all the while."

"How'd you..."

"Never mind. And I know that Sally's dead. I saw her hanging from a tree in the graveyard." He screwed up his face in disbelief and then blinked from the pain that caused. "The point is, Thomas, that I believed you. I believed you. I persuaded Will to go all over London and Southwark with me, looking for Sally, because I thought you were in love with the girl. Will and I spent hours together looking for her, and it was all for you." That last part wasn't entirely true. During most of my time with Will, I had hardly thought of my cousin, but Thomas deserved to squirm a bit for deceiving me. I folded my arms and stared down at him.

"I'm sorry, Lucy," he said softly. "I think we're both in danger now. Those two men, Jack and Patrick, they were trying to kill me, trying to keep me from finding whatever I could about Sally. You just happened to be with me the first time, but after tonight they're going to come after you, too. Lucy, promise me you'll be careful."

I laughed. "I don't think we have to worry about those two. They've been...shall we say...disarmed."

"Maybe, but whoever sent them this morning and again tonight, that person knew where to find me, knew where I'd be. Lucy, I'd feel better just knowing that you..."

"We're safe now, Thomas. Try to sleep." I stood up. I was suddenly very tired. "I'll come for you early, before Cook finds you here." I stepped to the door.

"If I could laugh right now," he said, "I would."

"What could possibly be funny?"

"You. You were mad enough to kill me, so you followed me. And that saved my life."

"Here," I said, pushing the sack of potatoes toward him with my foot. "A feather pillow, just for you."

When I reached my room, I did not even undress, but slid between the covers. Sleep would not come right away, and I stared out my window at the thousands of lights still burning in the city. This day, this once-hallowed English holiday that celebrated our patron saint, was done at last. Part of me wanted to stay awake, to think. There was much to think about. A girl had been murdered somewhere. Somewhere her murderer was roaming free. Tonight, I had almost become a murderer, myself. Somewhere in this enormous city, there was a man with eyes as black as onyx, a kind, intelligent, handsome man who had cheerfully spent two hours with me today. With me, Lucinda Culpeper.

No, Lucy, you're wrong, a voice said distinctly inside my head. That kind, intelligent, handsome man spent two hours with a boy—a boy named Luke.

And then the awfulness of what I had done struck me. I was angry with Thomas for lying to me, yet I had lied to Will from the moment we met. At least I had always known that Thomas was a spy. Will had no idea that I was really a girl. The lights outside the window seemed to dim. First thing tomorrow morning, I swore to myself, I would apologize to Thomas. But I could never apologize to Will.

The thought of him brought my mother's earrings to mind again. For the first time, I realized precisely what my theft

112

had accomplished: As long as my father lived, I could not wear those earrings in public. And in the same way, as long as I dressed as Luke, Will would never get to know Lucy. With a sigh, I closed my eyes. Suddenly everything was upside down and backwards.

I turned away from the window and heard a rustling sound under my pillow. Slipping my hand over the cool sheets, I came upon the rich damask of Sally's handbag. That note with its peculiar language jarred me wide awake. *The Bazile!* My eyes flew open. Now I knew what that meant. Backwards was the key.

I gripped the bag tightly and visualized the words. The Bazile was an almost perfect, backward-running anagram of the name *Elizabeth*. But surely, I told myself, surely this had nothing to do with Queen Elizabeth.

But if it did...

I would give the note to Thomas first thing in the morning.

Far in the distance, a church bell tolled the hour. I counted to twelve and took it for an omen. The hour was poised halfway between dark and dawn, just as I was teetering on the edge of understanding, on the brink of some great discovery, whether about myself or about the world, I had no clue. Perhaps, while I slept, the answer would come to me.

PART II

CHAPTER 6
THE LANGUAGE OF A SPY

April 24, 1589

I slipped downstairs before first light, but Thomas was already gone, apparently taking the table linens with him. *There* was a mystery that Cook would puzzle over the rest of the day. Since Father was gone also, I decided I might as well leave. When the sun came up, I was standing on a street in another part of London, looking up at Will's bedroom window. But there was no sign of him, and I had pelted the glass with pebbles. Will lived in respectable-looking surroundings. The walkways were swept clean. The red-roofed, two-story boardinghouse was well-kept. And the window glass was thick.

I scooped up another handful of pebbles, plucked out the biggest one and drew back my arm. Just before I let go, a movement at the side of the building caught my eye, ruining my aim. The rock hit someone else's window which then flew up like a startled guinea hen, and a scowling woman poked her head into the chilly air. In her hand was a pot of a type I recognized at once as a chamber pot. As I shot around the corner of the building, I was barely ahead of the pot's vile contents.

It seemed a fortunate turn of events when I noticed a man with a familiar gait walking half a block in front of me. He was gray-haired and dressed like a tradesman, wearing a plain, brown tunic and baggy leggings, but I saw

115

the glint of an earring when he turned the corner. I almost shouted his name.

Why didn't I? The truth was that I wanted to watch him, like a spy, unawares. Was that bizarre? In my own way, was I as strange as Ellen? I hoped not.

Nevertheless, follow him I did. And Father would have been proud of my stealth. Will's stride lengthened, and I had to run to keep him in sight. The shops were different now, with more taverns, more gaming houses. Then when he reached Speight Street, he halted. I hid behind a wooden column and watched him run up the steps of a two-story building with lace curtains at every window. The building had no sign, but above the door was the number 6, made of iron and about a foot high.

I drummed my fingers on the column's hard surface for a moment and then casually walked the distance to Number Four where a sign with three painted goblets announced what kind of place it was. Training my eyes on Number Six, I coolly folded my arms, leaned against a shutter and a split second later felt the pebbles of Speight Street gouging my backbone. How I got there is still a mystery, except for the vague memory of having my feet knocked out from under me. But I finally understood the phrase, "Keep an ear to the ground." In point of fact, that position enlivened all my senses.

"Ha! Now you don't look so smart, you little dandy."

I recognized the voice as Lord Pettigrew's, or Stephen Brooke, as he had introduced himself at the point of Will's sword. His boot obstructed my vision, resting as it did on

116

my windpipe, or I would've recognized his pretty face. Alas, my sword hand was pinned behind my back.

"Still lookin' for Sally, are you?"

"Mmph!"

"Speak up, you sneaky, hollow-eyed wretch," he shouted. "You're not her type, and neither is your friend. What did she tell you about me? I oughta..."

All at once I could breathe again. I closed my eyes and massaged my throat. When I opened my eyes, Stephen Brooke lay beside me on the street, and Will stood above him, applying his boot to Brooke's neck. I scrambled to my feet, unable to speak yet, but happy to breathe. As soon as I regained my voice, I planned to ask Will why he was wearing a patch over one eye, like a pirate.

"Once is excusable, sir," Will was saying, as he brandished his sword. "Twice makes a nasty habit." He threw me a one-eyed glance. "What do you say? A scar to remind him? Right about here?"

He poised the sword over Brooke's cheek, and the man's eyes studied the blade. Perhaps he recognized it. Perhaps he wanted it back.

"You there! Put up yer sword."

We looked toward Number Six. An enormous, bald fellow, nearly as wide as he was tall, filled the doorway. He was dressed in an Oriental get-up, a kind of long, orange nightgown that came just to the tips of his curly-toed shoes.

117

"I say there," the man called out, taking the stairs two at a time. "Whatta you think you're doin' in front o' this 'stablishment? Leave the gennulmun be."

When those Oriental shoes hit the street, Brooke probably felt the ground shake beneath his ear. Will sheathed his sword.

"Consider yourself rescued, Mr. Brooke. Next time? Who knows?"

He turned on his heel and strode away. I followed his lead. He did not look back.

After several blocks, Will halted. He leaned against the brick corner of a tailor's shop and began pulling off his eye-patch and wig. I stopped a few feet away and watched him stuff them into his tunic. Brooke had called Will my friend, but at the moment his dark eyes held an unfriendly gleam.

"What were you doing back there?" he asked.

"I ...uh...I went to your boardinghouse to...see if you'd go to Lord Wotton's with me."

"Your answer, as usual, begets more questions." He chewed on his lip for a moment. "How'd you know where I live?"

"You practically announced it yesterday," I said with a quick laugh, hoping he'd join in. 'I go to chapel every day,' you said. 'Sometimes twice a day.' And Mr. Taverner said that was only because you lived on Chapel Street. So when I got to Chapel Street, all I did was ask a man sweeping the walk in front of a building. He told me which apartment was yours. Upon my word, Will Shakespeare, word-play will get you in trouble someday."

"Sword-play certainly did that for me yesterday. Otherwise I wouldn't be here on a cold morning." He folded his arms and pinned me against the bricks with his gaze. "Now, what were you doing in the middle of Speight Street?"

"Brooke caught me off-guard while I was waiting for you. He must have come up on my left. For a big man, he's surpri..."

"No, no." Will held up his hand. His voice rose, too. "That isn't what I meant. How did you get from Chapel Street to Speight Street?"

"I...uh...I followed you."

"At last!" He slammed the palm of his hand against the side of the building. "A straight answer from a twisted mind. Now why...did...you...follow...me?"

Words fled my brain. The silence was actually painful. I was trapped in his black-eyed stare. "I don't know," I finally said.

"Finally, a statement I can believe." He laughed and clapped me on the shoulder as Thomas might have done. "Come along, Luke. Let's keep walking. You don't have to follow me, by the way. I will deign to let you walk beside me."

I sighed and fell in step.

"Tell me, Luke," he said after we had gone a block or two. "Do you know what kind of establishment Number Six Speight Street is?"

"It looked like a house, I guess."

"You're partly right," he said with a crooked smile. "I'll entertain you as we walk. Do you recall our discussion yesterday? The one about liberties and..."

I halted and gaped at him. "You mean..."

"Yes," he said, also stopping. "It's a brothel. Aren't you going to ask me what I was doing there?"

I gulped. "What you do is your own business."

"You followed me because you were curious. Weren't you curious about my disguise?"

I gulped again, afraid he'd ask about mine.

"Curiosity killed the cat, remember?" I shrugged and waved Will's question away as if I had not noticed his disguise. "I did not ask about it because...I'm...not a nosy person."

"Right. I believe you," he said with a wink and then grabbed me by the shoulder, pulling me along after him. "Let's put some more distance between us and that Oriental Gargantua."

As he walked, he took a card from his pocket and held it up for me to see. It was the one he found in Sally's handbag last night. *Peter Street 24* was written in thick script. Will turned the card over, and I saw that *Number Six Speight* was written in the same hand on the back. He tapped the words with his finger.

"I woke up during the night," he said, "intrigued by a remark you made."

He woke up and thought of me.

Biting my lip, I did a half-skip to catch up with him and gazed at the card.

"It was about the Single Woman's Graveyard," he went on. "You said you couldn't believe a girl would go there to commit suicide. She'd be admitting she was a prostitute, you said. What if Sally really was a prostitute, and her murderer knew it? Speight Street rang a bell. I'd overheard it somewhere. As it turns out, Mistress Payson, the proprietor of Number Six, knew Sally Clopton. A promising young woman, she called her, though she didn't exactly weep when I told her Sally was dead."

We passed a bakery, and I sneaked a glance at our reflections in the glass. Even in the baggy leggings, Will was the soul of elegance. He stopped to sniff the air, and so did I. Cinnamon! My empty stomach seemed to smell it, too, growling for my attention.

"I haven't had breakfast," Will said. "How about you?"

"No, but that reminds me. Here's what I owe you for the sausage." I pulled a coin out of my pocket. I had lifted it from Father's dressing table that morning. Father never gave me money of my own. It was one of the ways he controlled me.

Will threw me a puzzled look.

"On the bridge yesterday," I reminded him. "In exchange for the story about my great-uncle Thomas."

121

He nodded, stared at the coin a moment and then closed my fingers on it. "It was a good story. You earned the sausage."

Moments later, we were back on our way, each with our own loaf of cinnamon bread. We seemed to be going no place in particular. In his company, I didn't mind.

"Do you suppose Lord Pettigrew was one of Sally's customers?" I asked, breaking off a crusty corner. "Is that why he hung around Lord Wotton's yesterday and here at Number Six just now?"

"Good guess for someone who's not a nosy person. What did he say to you?"

"He called me a dandy and a sneaky, hollow-eyed wretch. He wanted to know if I was still looking for Sally. He wondered what Sally had told me about him, and then he told me I wasn't Sally's type."

"That's true enough," Will broke in.

"And he said you weren't, either."

He was about to pop a piece of bread into his mouth but stared at me instead. I looked away first, chomping down on the soft, warm center of the bread.

"Did you ever wonder, Luke, why young Lord Pettigrew did not tell us his full name?"

"Lots of reasons, probably. Maybe he thought we'd try to rob him if we knew he was a nobleman. Maybe..."

"Maybe he doesn't want word to get back to Papa Pettigrew that he's hanging around places he shouldn't, like Number Six Speight Street."

"Just curious. Is, uh, is it a hanging offense to have the pamphlet in your possession?"

"Will!" I halted and gripped his arm. "Tell me you haven't borrowed that book from somebody's library. Please tell me you've got more sense than that."

"No, I haven't borrowed that one yet. And yes, I have more sense." He grinned. "Does your hysteria mean it is a hanging offense?"

Hysteria! The disparaging word was always applied to women. I jerked my hand from his arm and spoke dispassionately, using my father as a model.

"It's a dangerous book even to discuss. It mocks the Queen and ridicules Lord Dudley, the man she loved. Almost always, the people who pass it around or keep it in their houses are traitors. If you were found with the pamphlet in your possession, you might not earn a hanging, but you might not recover from the interrogation, either." I shook my head, already tired of playing my father. "This conversation makes me nervous."

Will laughed. His smug expression was back. "Don't worry about me, Luke. I was just curious about the little green book. I'm not at all interested in activities that would —what was it our good Queen Bess said? *Activities that would separate a man from his shoulders."*

With a grin he reached out to pinch the skin at the base of my neck, and I raised my hand instinctively to my throat. The rustle of paper under my clothing startled me till I recalled what it was.

"Speaking of the Queen," I said, drawing the sheet from under my tunic, "remember this?"

He unfolded it, nodding slowly. "Yes, the bizarre note in Sally's purse."

"Yes. Look at the first two words and then read them backwards."

"Hmm. The first two, you said. *The Bazile*." His face darkened, and his eyes flew to mine. "This is the language of a spy, Luke. As I said last night, we should leave this for the authorities to investigate. If it leads to the Queen, then it leads back here, to the Tower."

The paper lay in his palm. The next moment, he might crumple it and drop it into the Thames. Already, he seemed to consider the paper his to destroy, the decision his to make, just like my father.

I snatched the paper from him and felt myself grow more inflamed with each word I said. "I won't give up that easily. Besides, I don't have anything else to do. I didn't get a job with your acting company, so I may as well become a spy. My family has connections. Who knows? Maybe I'll be the one to save the Queen."

I refolded the paper and slipped it back inside my tunic, aware that I had said too much, but too indignant, or too incensed by his roguish smile, to stop.

"See you onstage sometime, Will. Thanks for all the help."

I turned on my heel. He made no attempt to stop me.

Half an hour later, after wandering along the waterfront until I cooled down, I found myself at the rear of Lord Wotton's townhouse. At least I won't run into Patrick here, I told myself. Not after last night's encounter. As I rapped impatiently on the door, it occurred to me that after last night, Patrick would not be knocking on *any* doors for a while.

Alice opened the door. Her red curls were wilder than before.

"Hunh!" She laughed, angling her head at the wall behind her. "He said you'd be along."

"He?" I repeated. And there he stood, leaning against the opposite wall, his eyes as mysterious as the note from Sally's handbag.

"So," Alice went on, "now you finally seen her, didn't you?"

I turned away from him slowly. "Her?"

"Will told me," she said, cocking her head in his direction again. "What did you think? Was Sally as pretty as Thomas said?"

I shook my head. "No, she..."

"Hunh! That's one girl who earned her fate. Always off runnin' errands for his lordship, 'stead of stayin' here doin' her job."

Her eyes darted around the kitchen. "And now I got her work to do as well as mine. Lord knows, Sally never helped me any. She didn't want to ruin her hands. The only thing I could count on her to do was writin' the place

129

cards. She had a bee-you-di-ful handwritin'. Many's the time I wished I could write like her. Look at all these names I got to do for his lordship's dinner party tonight." She pulled a sheet of paper from her apron pocket and held it up for us to see.

Will peeled himself away from the wall. He still had not met my gaze, but he gave his full attention to the list in Alice's hand.

"You're in luck," he said. "The first time I met Luke, he told me he was very good at copying. I myself have no skill that way, but he's your man. Just bring on your place cards, and Luke will have 'em done in no time."

Alice clutched my arm, beaming as if I were an angel of mercy.

"Oh, Luke. That'd be a great help. You could sit right here. I'll bring everything to you." She ran to the hall door. "Lord Wotton has the prettiest standish you ever saw."

"Wait," Will called out. "What if his lordship comes in? We have no business in his..."

"Oh, he's not even here. Said he wouldn't be back for hours. Nobody's here but us. Stay there, and I'll fix some tea."

Still smiling, she closed the door behind her. I wasted no time.

"Why'd you come? You said..."

He put a finger to my lips.

"I think our Alice can neither read nor write. If you do this task, she'll answer any questions you have about Sally."

There were footsteps at the door, and Will rushed to open it. Alice bustled in, holding a gleaming standish filled with writing supplies.

"Here," she said, "look at the handle. I think it's gold. Run your fingers around it."

"It is a pretty one." I did as she said, but all I thought of was the way Will's finger had pressed against my lips.

"Here," she went on, "this bowl's for ink, of course, and the others, well, you know what they're for. Do you need anything? Here's the guest list. I'll fix that tea."

She scurried off, afraid perhaps that I'd ask for something outside her knowledge. Leaning decoratively against the door leading to the hall, Will gave me an encouraging nod. I sat at the table and picked up the pen. At the hearth, chattering like a bird, Alice set some water to boil and began kneading pie shells. Behind me, Will whistled a tune under his breath. After the morning's strange events, I found I was glad to sit and be quiet. I practiced awhile, but only a few minutes of work produced, in my opinion, an acceptable rendition of Lord Wotton's name. I held the card up for them to admire.

"Aw, that's bee-you-di-ful," Alice said, walking up beside me.

"It's called the secretary hand. What do you think, Will?" I turned around and dropped the card to the table. He no longer decorated the door.

"Where'd he go?" Alice asked.

"Oh," I said, hesitating only the tiniest instant, "he must have run outside again. He told me one time that...that... when he was a boy, his parents apprenticed him to work at an inn. Now he can't abide the smell of food cooking. Says it makes him ill."

"Hunh! First it was a church. Now it's an inn. He's an odd one."

I agreed wholeheartedly. And silently hoped that he wouldn't get caught. Someday his love for other men's books would get him in trouble. Meanwhile, I'd have to ask questions of Alice all by myself. This just proved what I'd come to believe about men: they are generally unreliable creatures.

I turned out place cards while Alice turned out pies. We talked, but I learned nothing of value. Now that the news about Sally had sunk in, Alice seemed reluctant to say anything else about the girl, good or bad. When the hall door opened, I glanced up angrily, ready to blast Will for abandoning me.

A stranger stood there, a tall, older man with the bold stare and bearing of a soldier.

"Alice, what's going on here?"

"Oh, Lord Wotton," Alice said, bringing a floury hand to her face.

Oh, Lord, I said to myself and scrambled to my feet.

"Sir, there's bad news. Sally's dead. This young man came, sir." She put a hand on my arm. "He came by to tell me that somebody murdered Sally."

His lordship's face registered mild surprise. It was not a handsome face, older than I had imagined, black-eyed and sharp-featured like a hawk.

"Murder, you say? What a pity!" A strand of gray-streaked hair fell across his forehead, and he brushed it back irritably. "Now I suppose I'll have to get Basset to hire more help."

He turned his hawk-like stare on me. Only then did I notice his lordship's barrel-like chest, his saber-straight posture and the fact that his piercing eyes bored into mine from a height of several inches.

"And who are you?"

A phrase from Greek literature came to my mind, but the English translation carries more force: *Kill the messenger.* Only the seat of the chair, pressing against my knees, kept me from taking a backward step.

"I, I'm a friend of Sally's, sir. I thought Alice should know what happened."

"But what are you doing at my table. And with my standish?"

"It was my idea, sir," Alice said, her floury hand gripping my arm. "I asked him to label the place cards, since Sally isn't here."

"Oh, that reminds me." He reached into a pocket. "Here are the names of two other guests. I'll likely have several more names later."

He threw a sheet of paper onto the table and angled his head to inspect my handiwork. The motion sent a whiff of whiskey my way.

"Those are quite good. Where did you learn the bastard hand?"

He gave me a look of disbelief. I felt like a mongrel dog caught skulking away with a piece of the family silver.

"Thank you, sir," I said modestly. "A cousin taught me."

"I could use you right away," Lord Wotton went on, gesturing at the food that was in various stages of preparation all over the kitchen. "You could help Alice. Here's a shilling for the work you've done so far. We'll see how you do tonight."

My refusal must have seemed unlikely, for he turned away as soon as he put the coin on the table.

"I'll be in the library, Alice. I don't want to be disturbed."

The door swung shut behind him. The library! I gripped the table edge in alarm, certain that Will's luck was about to run out.

I sat at the table and absently picked up the pen, my thoughts only on Will as my fingers mechanically moved it across a place card. Should I try to warn him? How?

"Your friend Will could get a job as a spy," Alice said.

Damn! I reached for the bowl of pounce to blot a splotch of ink.

"I sure didn't see 'im leave," she added.

"When I finish these," I said, "I think I'll step out into the alley for some air."

The door to the alley creaked open just then, and the gray cat streaked in, straight for its bowl of food in a corner. The door opened all the way, and Basset entered. The stare he threw me was every bit as black as his gaze had been yesterday, but today one of his eyes was also black. Since yesterday, Basset's left eye had come in contact with a very powerful force. I stared back, unable to hide a smile, and he wiped his feet noisily.

"Alice," he said in a sharp voice, "you know his lordship don't like riffraff in the kitchen. What is he doin' here?"

"Lord Wotton's paid him to letter those cards. Besides, this is my kitchen. What do you want?" Alice did not even look up from the apple she was peeling. Basset had stationed himself in front of the copper pot hanging by the door, and he was admiring his thick, black hair in its shiny surface.

"I say, where's Sally? Doin' them cards is her job."

Alice sighed and tossed the apple into a nearby washtub where it rolled around like a cannonball. "Sally never helped me, Basset. You know that. Besides, Sally's dead. Luke here came to tell me that somebody killed her."

He wheeled around, looking astonished, much more than Lord Wotton had been. His bushy eyebrows shot up.

135

"I say, do they know who done it?"

"No," Alice said, again without looking up. "She was strangled."

He grimaced. "His lordship won't like that at all. Not the least little bit, I should say. He fancied Sally."

"His lordship already knows, Basset. I just told him."

"His lordship's back already?"

She nodded. "Said he was goin' to the library and didn't want to be disturbed."

"That's not good." He cleared his throat and went back to his image in the copper pot. "I have to see 'im. If I don't hire extra help soon, I'll have to take what I can get."

"But isn't that what his lordship pays you for, Basset? To do things he doesn't want to do? To make his life easier?" Alice glanced up long enough to toss another apple into the washtub.

"You don't understand this sort o' business, woman." He gave her a patronizing smile. "His lordship must tell me how many servants and at what price. It's standard practice."

She shrugged. "Hire all you need. If it's too many, pay 'em out of your own big salary that I'm always hearin' about." Figuring she had the last word, she moved to a table near the window.

I looked at Basset from under my lashes. He studied the back of Alice's head for a moment, formed his fists into hammerheads and then quickly, wordlessly, opened the door. At the last moment, the cat decided to leave the kitchen, too, and Basset kicked at it. Its screech echoed down the hallway.

As the door closed, Alice swung around to face me, smiling as if we were conspirators, or worse yet, sweethearts. That did it. Standing up, I put the pen down so hard the nib broke, and then I stuffed my trembling hands into my pockets and began to move slowly toward the rear door.

"What are you making now?" I asked, mostly to cover my movements.

She chopped away at a big, white onion on the countertop. In spite of her smile, tears were beginning to run down her face. "Onion soup," she said, with a nod at the bunch of small onions beside her. "And then I'll take them leeks."

With a grin, I opened the door to the alley.

"I think," I said, "I think I'll just take a leak, too."

Her cheeks turned as red as her hair.

I closed the door and ran down the alley. When I reached the front of the house, I crouched behind a row of shrubs and crept along till I passed under an open window. The day was fair and warm, and several windows along the front stood open. Had I come far enough? Will had mentioned that the library was down the hall and on the left, past the huge banquet hall. What if I poked my head up and locked eyes with someone in the wrong room?

Slowly I raised my head and quickly lowered it. A noise, a kind of rustling sound in the street, made me wheel in that direction. Through the shrubs that concealed me, I saw a man walking toward Lord Wotton's house. Walking is

137

not quite the right word. He reached out with one foot to stab the ground, and then he dragged the other foot up to join it. He was a very old man, bearded and wild-eyed, with mottled, purple blotches on his face. Dressed as he was in a torn, gray shirt and blue woolen pants, I took him to be a wounded veteran. Many of them roamed London's streets, though usually not in neighborhoods like Lord Wotton's.

From inside the room above me, a door opened.

"Ah, there you are," someone said. Was that Basset's voice?

The old man drew closer. Above me, I heard the hum of another voice and wanted desperately to peer into the room. Was it the library? Had Will been caught stealing a book? The old fellow made it as far as the stairs leading to the front door where he threw himself onto the bottom step, clinging to the railing. Less than ten feet away, I watched his bruised and haunted eyes flit up and down the street. Those eyes. There was something about those...

It was Thomas! What was he up to? The same thing as me? Looking for Sally's murderer?

All at once, he lurched up from the bottom step and began to make his way to the other end of the street. I watched him till he disappeared around the corner. I did not want to think about how angry he'd be if he saw me here.

Cautiously, I stood on tiptoe and lifted my head above the windowsill. A multi-colored tapestry dominated the wall to my left, but floor-to-ceiling shelves on either side of it were filled with books. In random places, marble and brass sculptures served as bookends. Well, Lucy, I said to myself, you found the library all right. Now I understood why Will had felt that borrowing one little book did not matter so much.

Afraid to move any part of my body rapidly, I scanned the wall slowly and froze in place. A face was staring at me from a shelf very close to the window, a chalky-white face with an unnatural gaze. In spite of myself, I blinked and then almost laughed in relief. The face was only a marble head-and-shoulders sculpture of the Greek poet Homer. Father had a similar one in his study.

I resumed my scan. Everywhere, shelves bulged with books and sculptures and swords in ornamental scabbards. In the center of the wall opposite the window was a fireplace, but shelves of books covered every other inch of space. I drew in my breath. Lord Wotton sat in a high-backed chair near the tapestry, directly across from my window. His feet rested on an ottoman, and the fingers of one hand held a wineglass. Basset stood respectfully at his side. They had not seen me yet, nor had I seen Will. Perhaps I should search another room, before my luck ran out.

I half-turned away at the exact moment that Lord Wotton glanced up and cocked his head in my direction. Now I dared not move a hair.

"Whatever you think," Lord Wotton said. "I'm sure you'll do the right thing."

"Well, sir, I thank you for sayin' so. It's just that this is such an important dinner party tonight, sir. I wanted to be sure we have enough servants."

"I'm sure it will be fine, Basset," Lord Wotton said. "Lady Sophie was always pleased with the arrangements you made for her parties. Just serve me as well."

Lady Sophie. I recalled the inscription in the book Will had taken from this room.

"Yes, sir, I'll do my best," Basset said.

"That reminds me. When you hire a replacement for Sally, find someone who'll do a better job with my wife's things. Lady Sophie was always very particular about her possessions." Lord Wotton addressed his remarks to his wine glass, and it occurred to me that he had probably not yet seen Basset's black eye. Perhaps this was why Basset had not bothered to cover the bruise with makeup. I recalled that Father never made eye contact with our servants, either. Basset abruptly reached for the bottle of wine.

"Lady Sophie was a woman of *esquizzit* taste, your lordship," Basset said, refilling his lordship's glass.

"Aye," Lord Wotton agreed, "the best woman who ever lived."

His lordship gazed intently at the far wall near the door. Craning my neck to the right, I saw a portrait of a stern-faced but beautiful woman. Father had told me that Lord Wotton was a widower, but somehow, at least when Lord Wotton spoke of her, Lady Sophie did not seem entirely dead.

"She was the queen of my heart," he added, raising his glass. "I'm just not sure she'd approve of this party so soon after ..."

"Now, sir," Basset said soothingly. "It's been a full year. Lady Sophie would 'a wanted you to go on with life."

I hardly believed this was the same man who made fists behind Alice's back, the same man who called me riffraff and kicked at a cat.

Lord Wotton set the glass down quickly. Drops of wine splashed onto his white shirt.

"Oh, sir," Basset said. "Sorry to upset you. Let me refill that glass."

Lord Wotton stood up, dabbing at the shirt with his hands, spreading the stain even more. Abruptly, he broke off, stared up at the portrait once more and stalked toward the door. He put his hand to the latch.

"I know you had my interests at heart, Basset," his lordship said, "but this party just doesn't feel right. It's too soon. I want you to send word to the guests. I'm calling it off."

"Whatever you say, sir. Basset glanced up at Lady Sophie's portrait. "Still, I doubt her ladyship would approve 'a wastin' all that food."

Lord Wotton narrowed his hawk-like eyes and gazed at her portrait also. "Hmm. That is a point. She was a very frugal woman." He slowly nodded his head. "Proceed, then. Hire any number of servants you need. I'll change my shirt and come back down."

"Yes, sir," Basset said dutifully.

The door closed. Basset waited for a moment and then moved quietly to his lordship's chair and halted before the ottoman. Lifting off the padded lid, he peered inside. A smile transformed his face, and he chuckled.

"Lady Sophie always were a *partickler* woman," he said, as if speaking to someone inside the ottoman. "Very partickler and very frugal. And so am I. A place for everything, I always say."

I blinked in surprise, unsure who was the greater eccentric, Lord Wotton or his servant. I slumped to the ground and hurried away. When I slipped into the kitchen again, Alice looked up shyly.

"Did you run into your friend?"

"No no, I didn't."

"Well, don't forget those other names his lordship give you."

"Right!" I had to earn that shilling. I sat down and pulled the sheet toward me. Perhaps Will had gone on to the theater, the scoundrel. Unfolding the paper, I saw that there were only two names on the list, but they were the last two I would ever have expected to see: Lord Edward Culpeper and Lady Lucinda Culpeper. Father and I, guests at Lord Wotton's party?

I sharpened the nib of the pen I'd slammed down earlier. Had Father wangled this invitation solely because I mentioned Lord Wotton's name last night? Years ago, when I wanted to study Latin under a more learned teacher, Father refused. Last year, when I wanted to stop studying the wretched harpsichord, he refused. This year, when I wanted to visit Thomas in France, he refused. Of all times for

Father to do something because he thought I might want it, now was not the time I'd choose.

Writing these two names took longer than it should have. I was worried about Will and bewildered about Thomas, but Alice bent my ear talking about her family. I found we had something in common, though I couldn't tell her so. We both had spent our childhood at Tintabeney! Her father had been a cobbler on my family's estate. And now we both were here in London, trying to make a living.

I was just dotting the letter *i* in the name Lucinda, when the rear door opened. Alice and I turned at the same time. Will stood on the threshold.

"We have to go, Luke. Now."

His face, drawn and unsmiling, persuaded me as much as his voice. I figured he must be late for rehearsal. Alice frowned.

"Here," I said, tossing her the shilling. "Sorry, but I can't work tonight."

The door slammed shut behind us. Will set off toward the theater at a rapid pace, and I jogged to keep up. We moved so fast as to make speech difficult. Finally though, I could stand it no longer.

"Where'd you go, Will?"

He cut his eyes toward me but said nothing.

"Never mind. I'd rather not know," I said, speaking in ragged phrases as I ran. "Let me tell you what I did. I went out the back door, looking for you. I didn't find you, of course, but I did spy on Lord Wotton and Basset in the library. You won't believe how...peculiar those two are. Lord Wotton is quite the grieving widower, and Basset coddles him like a baby."

"That does sound very peculiar."

Will made a clucking noise in his throat and stared at the dust his boots kicked up.

"That isn't the half of it," I went on. "When Lord Wotton left the room, Basset opened up his lordship's ottoman and began speaking to it. You'd have thought..."

"Permit me," Will interrupted. "Showing is far superior to telling."

He came to an abrupt halt in front of a tailor's shop and bent forward to peer at the garments hanging in the window. I stopped also, wondering what in the world he had in mind.

"Lady Sophie always were a *partickler* woman," he said to the garments. "Very partickler and very frugal. And so am I. A place for everything, I always say." Then Will stood up straight and glanced at me, his dark eyes dancing.

"How did you know that? I asked.

"Maybe I'm simply very clever," he said, folding his arms. "Isn't that why you asked me to help you look for Sally? Because I'm so clever?"

"You were hiding in that room. Where?"

"It may seem cowardly to you," he said with a laugh, "but when I heard a noise at the door, I ran to the—what do you call one of those wall-sized tapestries?"

"An arras?"

144

He nodded. "That's right. Anyway, when I heard a noise at the door, I just had time to jump behind the arras. The cloth is eaten up with little moth holes, and I was afraid I'd be discovered. But it has some convenient slits just at eye-level, and I could see."

"Why do you take such risks, Will?"

"And you don't?"

"Not for books," I snapped.

"You think that's why I went back to the library?"

"Isn't it?

He shrugged. "Alice said Lord Wotton wouldn't be back for hours. She said no one else was at home. Besides, some things are worth any risk. But enough of the library. While we walk, tell me what happened when I was out of the kitchen."

I told him everything I could think of: what Alice had said about Lord Wotton, what his lordship had said about Sally, and what Basset had said about both of them. Each man had seemed surprised that Sally was dead.

"Is there anything else?" Will asked. I shook my head, but he shook his harder. His golden earring swung wildly. "You seem to be holding something back," he said. "But you've been like that since early morning." He tapped his chin.

I hesitated. I had already told him too much. "I might become a spy," I had said. "My family has connections," I had said. How much can I trust him, I wondered. Could I tell him about Jack and Patrick beating Thomas last night?

145

Could I tell him that I had come close to killing both men? Would I really have run them through, I asked myself.

His eyes seemed to follow my circuitous reasoning. Tell me what you are thinking, those eyes said. And so I told him. Not everything, not about Father or Thomas's work, but about the fight in the dark street. I told him how Jack, at sword point, was ready to explain the word *rosemary* but Patrick had stopped him. All Will did, really, was nod and crinkle his intelligent eyes. He may have thought I was making it all up, especially the story of how I single-handedly rescued Thomas and disarmed both men. I suddenly wished I had not said a word.

A light rain began to fall.

I laughed, looking up into the gray sky and glad for an interruption. "Will this cancel this afternoon's play?"

"Perhaps not. As an actor, I've learned not to worry about the rain. It's one of the things I let God manage."

"Magnanimous of you. Be that as it may, a cancellation would be disastrous."

He lifted his eyebrow. "You're not appearing in this play, are you?"

"Wish I were, but during the play I had planned to study some minor suspects, Arthur Clopton and Gilbert Dereham."

When we reached the theater, the rain had slowed to a fine mist. I would have loved to remove my cap, for it seemed to channel the water down my cheeks and into my ears. Very soon, though, my ears were full of something else. Shouting, shrieks and sobbing issued from the vicinity of the stage.

"That can't be a rehearsal going on," I said. "There's none of that noise in today's play."

"You know *Love's Last Lament*?"

"I've seen it dozens of times. Know it by heart."

One look at the stage solved the mystery. A tall, middle-aged woman stood in the center, holding Arthur Clopton by one ear; she was screaming into the other.

"This wicked worl' has taken one o' my children from me. I'll not let it take another. You're comin' home with me, young sir. Now!"

Arthur tried valiantly to resist, but his mother had the strength of grief on her side. She dragged him to the rear of the stage while most of the troupe stood by helplessly.

"And as for you," she said, turning her red-eyed stare on Mr. Bright. "You and your company is responsible for my daughter's murder. She'd been comin' round to see your plays, quite regular, I hear, and look what happent to 'er."

Robert Taverner ran to block the doorway, but Mrs. Clopton charged toward him, towing Arthur like a horse pulling a plow.

"Now, ma'am," Taverner said, swerving to the side as she swept past, "what you say is motivated by grief and not by reason. Surely you understand that Arthur depends on his job here for his livelihood? And we depend on his performance. He's a valuable member of our ensemble. While I certainly sympathize..."

"Sympathize? I'll not have your sympathy, you scoundrelly man. You've turned aside this sweet, upstandin' boy of mine. It'll take prayer and fastin' to turn 'im round again."

The sweet, upstanding boy was in danger of losing an ear.

"Let's go, Arthur," she said, as if he had a choice.

And so, with the boy whimpering and Mrs. Clopton dragging him across the wooden stage and yelling Scripture at him the whole while, the two departed.

Robert Taverner slapped his hands together and stomped the floor angrily.

"That woman is a holy virago! What's left for us, now? Pray for more rain?"

"There's only one thing to do," Will said, walking toward the steps at stage right. "Be grateful that Luke here knows the play by heart. He can take over Arthur's roles, and he'll do a damned fine job, I'll warrant."

Well, there it was. Exactly what I'd wanted, a chance to perform with this company.

I'd just always thought I'd have more time to prepare.

CHAPTER 7
THE CODE IS BROKEN

That afternoon, I got what I had always wanted: the chance to act on a stage.

Was I wonderful? With no rehearsal and less than one hour's preparation, there's no sense pretending that my performance was anything more than ordinary. And under the circumstances, ordinary was truly wonderful.

I played several roles, of course, but my favorite was as the maid named Thalia. *Love's Last Lament* is only a silly romance, yet the finale has two of the three elements, according to Will, which are necessary to a happy ending, the three elements being (in no particular order): the wicked are punished, the good are rewarded, and the pretty girls get kissed. In *Love's Last Lament,* only the final one is missing.

Taking a bow in Thalia's costume as hundreds of people clapped and cheered was a singular thrill, though I suppose it would be remarkable if even one among them had singled out my performance.

As I rose from my second bow, I noticed one face in particular, a very pretty one, though it was on a man's body. Stephen Brooke sat in the lower gallery, beside a girl whose face was largely hidden. As she whispered in his ear, I thought he might have been staring directly at me, a thought confirmed when the girl turned to me and smiled knowingly. Her face exposed, I now knew who she was, and my scalp did crawl. It was Ellen.

149

Gilbert Dereham unceremoniously dragged me off the stage, a gesture I deeply resented. My bows were no longer than anyone else's.

"Apparently, London's *hoi polloi* love you," Gilbert said. "The groundlings certainly know talent when they see it. Oh, but perhaps I said it wrong." He brought his hand with its gaudy, jeweled rings to his cheek. "May I say *the* when I speak of groundlings?" he asked, without a trace of a smile. Abruptly, he turned on his heel.

I stood perfectly still, staring at his wide backside as he waddled toward the 'tiring room, and I wondered how a grown man could hang onto such a silly grudge. And all I did, I told myself, was correct his use of a Greek phrase. Or was he jealous of my sudden good fortune? Thomas had warned me about actors' jealousies. Someone patted me on the back, and I wheeled around, startled. It was Mr. Bright.

"Wonderful job, Luke," he said. "Are you familiar with the play we're performing tomorrow, *And Sooner Make An End?*"

"Yes, sir. I've seen it several times. With a small amount of study, I can be ready with Arthur's roles well in time for the performance," I added and then held my breath.

"Come back tomorrow. If Arthur doesn't show up, you're on."

"Yes, sir!"

"A warning, though." He held up a finger like a school-master. "The other theater owners in London will turn a

150

blind eye to misbehavior. I do not. An actor who's out carousing at night won't give a good performance the next day. And there's the London Council to consider. They would be only too happy to close our theater down if one of our number gets himself in trouble. They already believe that actors cause most of the ills in this city. Remember that," he said and patted me on the back once more.

Bright was still in his costume, a long, flowing, white robe. With his silver hair and kindly smile, he looked like God incarnate. I'd have promised him my first-born son.

"You can count on me, sir."

Robert Taverner clapped me on the shoulder then, almost knocking me down.

"Good work, young fellow."

After a couple more minutes backstage, though, I was completely ignored. So much for my big debut. I tromped off to the 'tiring room to change clothes, discreetly, of course.

I tried to time my costume-changing so that Gilbert Dereham and I would walk toward the exit together. Because he's so wide, I didn't speak till we had left the narrow hall. I wanted to see his face clearly.

"Gilbert," I said. "It's too bad about Sally, isn't it?"

"Sally who?" He didn't slow down.

"Sally Clopton. Arthur's sister."

"What about her?"

"She's dead. Didn't you know?"

He shook his head and reached up to twirl his long mustache.

"How'd it happen?"

"They say she was hanged."

I studied his eyes for a clue. And then I recalled he was an actor, trained to mask his own feelings and show feelings not his own.

"I'd be willing to bet she deserved it," he said without changing his expression. "That girl has made plenty of men angry enough to kill her."

Then he was out the door and immediately got lost among a dozen screaming women. He threw a glove into the air and halted to see who caught it. The lucky lady was a blonde in a red dress, none other than Ellen Beddoes, Thomas's old girlfriend, and most recently seatmate of Stephen Brooke. I leaned forward, watching her walk away with Dereham. His courting procedure was just that simple.

"Who are you looking at?"

I wheeled around. Will stood in the middle of the stage. Everyone else seemed to have gone.

"Dereham and Ellen Beddoes, of all people." I rolled my eyes and took a few steps toward him. "I can't imagine those two together. Just now, Dereham told me that Sally deserved to die. I can't help but wonder if..."

"Don't."

"Don't what?"

"Don't wonder about Sally. Leave it to a constable."

I cocked my head. Was he serious?

"Why give up now?" I asked. "We're close. I can feel it."

"Stop now, Luke," he said, his dark eyes pinning me to the spot. "Or the only thing you'll feel will be the murderer's fingers around your own throat."

I shook my head in puzzlement. "If you weren't interested in this mystery, why'd you spend the whole morning running all over London with me? The time you owed me has long since expired."

"That in itself is a mystery," he said, holding my gaze and beginning to walk around me to the back of the stage. His hands were clasped behind his back, and he kept his voice low. "I suppose because it's been fun, in a nerve-tingling way. Like being onstage, in a play that the writer hasn't quite finished yet."

I watched him warily. He seemed to be moving closer, but in a circular motion. The props from the afternoon production littered the stage: a few weapons, a three-legged stool, a small table, a book. He skirted all of them gracefully.

"It has been fun," I said, turning as I spoke to keep him in view. "So why quit now?"

He showed no sign of hearing me, though he never took his eyes from mine, the circle growing ever smaller.

"You're something of an unfinished play yourself, Luke. You're rather nerve-tingling to be around, and there's more to you than meets the eye. Do you recall the play I'm writing?"

"Of course," I snapped. I'd soon be dizzy with this blasted turning. "The one you call *The Comedy of Terrors*."

"*Errors*," he said with the smallest of smiles. "It was my play that started all of this, you know. It began with that first innocent question that Taverner asked, the question you so cleverly answered. It was *The Brothers Menaechmi,* you said."

He was almost near enough to touch me, yet he continued circling me slowly, all the while staring with those impossibly dark eyes.

"Have I ever told you what my play is about, in one or two words, I mean?"

I shook my head.

"A playwright should be able to do that, I think, to use only a few words to describe his whole story. This comedy, as I call it, is a riot of confusing actions, but they all arise from one simple occurrence. It's like a full, ripe peach around that single, hard pit at the center."

"What is it about?" My voice was a whisper.

"Mistaken identity."

And then he stopped circling. No one else was in the entire theater, and he was near, quite near. It was hard for me to breathe. All I could see was my reflection in his onyx eyes. I flung out my hand to steady myself and caught his arm.

"My word!" I cried, with a nervous laugh. "What's this on your wrist?"

"What?" A smile played at the corner of his mouth.

"This bump on the back of your hand. How did you get that?"

He flexed the fingers of his right hand, and a bump as big as a pea wiggled around under the skin of his wrist. Now he laughed outright.

"It's rather charming, don't you think? One of these always springs up after I use a sword. I suppose I can blame you for this one. I noticed it after yesterday's sword fight. It'll go away in a day or two."

"Don't blame me," I shot back. "The swordplay was your idea. Does it hurt?"

"No, but it makes my fingers go numb when I've been writing for awhile. The handwriting suffers, but at least I can read what I've written."

I examined the raised skin. "It looks like a Bible bump."

"What's that? One of the plagues of Egypt?"

I scanned the stage and dragged him to the nearby table.

"No, it's a bump that can be healed with a Bible. Put your hand here," I said, bending down to pick up the big book from the floor.

"That isn't a Bible. It's only a block of wood carved to look like a book."

"So it is," I said, hefting it. "Ought to work. The main thing is to use a big book. Most of the time, that would be a Bible. Just hold your hand still. It won't hurt much. I've seen my father's servant do this for the cook." I held the block of wood high above his hand and dropped it to the table, but he was halfway to the door when it hit.

"Why'd you move?" I yelled after him. "I was going to heal you."

"Saint Luke may have been a physician, but I refuse to let his namesake operate on me."

He exited through the main gate, avoiding the screaming horde behind the stage, and I thought it appropriate to follow. The Bible bump had worked as well as anything to change an awkward subject. *Mistaken identity*, indeed, I thought. That was getting a bit close for comfort. Will may not have noticed, but I did not drop the block of wood until he had jerked his hand away.

By the time I reached him, we were almost alone on the street. I had no idea where he was going, but I had nowhere to be until Lord Wotton's dinner party at eight.

"Listen," I said, as if nothing had happened. "About that card we found in Sally's handbag, the one that had Number Six Speight and Peter Street 24 written on it. You found Speight Street, and number six is the brothel, but I don't recall ever coming across Peter Street, and I'm a native Londoner." I skipped to keep up with his longer stride and glanced up at him. He was frowning at me.

"I was serious, Luke. You should stop prying into Sally's murder, or you will be hurt."

"Ha! And I thought you were joking."

"Real, live men don't joke in the face of death, Luke. Only actors."

He spoke without turning to look at me. That, more than his words, set me off. I halted in the middle of the street.

"You are a coward, Will Shakespeare."

He stopped. The sudden tensing of his shoulders should have warned me.

"Things get a little ticklish," I went on, "and you run away."

The hand with the Bible bump flashed out to grab my collar, and instantly my feet left the ground. His face was inches from mine, his mustache nearly brushing my cheek. His voice became a whisper.

"You told me about your Great-uncle Thomas and that skull of his on a pike high above the bridge. It was a *memento mori*, you said, a reminder to citizens that they, too, must die." He paused as if waiting for a response, but all I could do was nod my head. "Let it be a *memento mori* to yourself, Luke."

He paused again, and I swallowed hard.

"Do you recall the man we saw today?" he went on. "The man on his way to the Tower?"

"Are you t-trying to frighten me?"

"No, you don't have enough sense to be frightened. But I do. That man on his way to the Tower may have children. They'll soon be fatherless. I won't do that to my children. Do you understand?"

He studied my face and then, with a slow smile, he dropped me gently to the ground. Perhaps I should have held my tongue.

"You rarely talk about your children," I said. "And never about your...wife."

The instant I spoke the last word, his face darkened. For a long moment, he regarded me coldly. His voice, when he finally spoke, was hard as ice.

"Sometimes, Luke, sometimes a man finds himself framed into serving a different kind of sentence." He turned and walked away, flinging his last words over his shoulder. "A life sentence."

I stared after him, feeling guilty for what I had said. He was moving farther away, blending in with the crowd, but I shrugged. I knew I would see him again. After all, we now worked at the same theater.

Reaching up to smooth my collar, I heard a rustling under my tunic and pulled out a sheet of paper, the one from Sally's handbag. Seeing it for the first time in the light of day, I realized that the writer had used the old-fashioned, secretary style of handwriting. The cryptic words leaped out at me: *The Bazile*. Had I guessed right? Was this a code word for the Queen?

I glanced down the street, but Will was nowhere in sight. I tapped the sheet against my palm. Most likely, Father could break the code in short order, but he would certainly persist in discovering how I came by it. And I most definitely could not confess that I'd found it in a dead girl's handbag.

But I did have one other resource at my disposal, at least when I dressed as a woman: Father's assistant, Henry Rendle, the young Lord Winter.

Half an hour later, having stopped at home for a costume change, I approached Henry's townhouse, while the sun was still above London's roofline. Nevertheless, my mood was dark. I have loathed few things more than the prospect of seeking a favor from a man who so consistently sought my own favor.

A servant answered the bell immediately, took my calling card and led me into a small parlor. Henry appeared a moment later, as if he'd been waiting for me.

He was wearing a thick, white collar at his neck and smaller, white ruffs at his wrists. His doublet, sleeves, breeches, and hose were black. This two-tone apparel mirrored Henry's own coloring. His skin was pale because he rarely went out in the daytime, and a thin, black mustache only accented his pallor. His flat, black eyes were arresting enough, but Henry's voice was the most peculiar part of the man. It did not vary more than two tones when he spoke. The house could be on fire, yet his warning might be in the same voice he would use to offer more tea.

"Lucinda," he greeted me. "You look lovely in that dress. Green is your color. Are you really alone? You have never come to see me alone. How remarkable."

"I have a paper to show you, Henry."

Immediately, I reached for it in my bag. Otherwise, he'd take my fingers and wrap them around his forearm.

"I found this yesterday, Henry. Where I found it doesn't matter, but I'd like your opinion. Decode it if you can, please. It looks as if it's in code."

He studied it for a moment, and I realized that I had never seen his eyes flicker with light until now.

"Hmm. Very odd handwriting, that much is clear. You may have noticed that it is not in one particular style either because the writer wanted to disguise his own script or because he has a vacillating mind. As for the words themselves, I see no bizarre symbols or arcane runes. Those usually point toward an incredibly difficult code. I wonder if this is connected with a lead I was following. Hmm." He rubbed his thin mustache and abruptly seemed to notice me again. "I'll see what I can do, Lucinda, but don't worry your pretty little head over this. I'm sure it has nothing to do with anything important."

He was too fast for me. My hands were no longer busy with the letter. Before I could stop him, he appropriated one of them to drape across his forearm.

"How do you plan to repay me for this favor?" he asked and raised an eyebrow in what he probably thought was a clever expression.

"Oh, perhaps I'll play the harpsichord for you sometime, Henry." My voice was beginning to imitate his own limited range. "Do you suppose I might drop by tomorrow to learn what the letter means? Would that give you enough time?"

"For you, Lucinda, I'll do it today. Will you be at home later?"

I slid my hand from his arm. "Until a little before eight, I think. Father is taking me somewhere tonight."

"Good," he said and crinkled his eyes in what he probably thought was a very tender look. "I like to know that you venture out from time to time, Lucinda. I do hate to think of you always staying in that big house, reading or sewing

160

or playing the harpsichord. Is your father taking you to Tintabeney this summer?"

Henry's family had an estate not far away from Tintabeney. Not far enough away, I feared.

"I don't know, Henry," I said, backing away from him as much as I could without seeming to back away. "Father has been very busy lately. In fact, please don't tell him about this paper. I don't want to bother him. And now, I'd best be going. Thank you for agreeing to read that. It may be nothing at all. I hope so," I added with a shrug.

"I'll walk you to the door," he said, crinkling his eyes again and taking my hand.

As he opened the door, a butterfly flew in, and I stepped back, startled. It may have been startled also, for it flew straight toward Henry. Reaching out two fingers, he picked it up in flight, holding it by one wing. The butterfly was a beautiful, iridescent blue, and I was hypnotized for a moment that such an ethereal creature was actually in London and in Henry's hand.

Not for long. First, he pulled off the antennae, one by one. Then each wing *snap, snap* until only the tiny, trembling body remained. Without glancing where it would land, he tossed the dismantled butterfly out the door and bent to kiss my hand. I stared at the top of his head. And I had thought Thomas's old girlfriend Ellen was strange. Ellen was only as surprising as a cellar in the dark. Henry's oddities would have filled a castle.

I said good-bye and walked down the stairs, picking up my skirt and mindful of where I stepped. It was quite easy now to imagine Henry engaging in an occasional scraping of the soul at the Tower. With these unpleasant thoughts, it's understandable why I was not on my guard as I turned the corner at the end of the street.

"En garde!" a familiar voice called out.

I whipped my head from side to side. To my left, less than three feet away, stood Stephen Brooke, his pretty face wreathed in a smile.

"Catch."

He tossed me a sword. I caught it by the grip and realized two things: this was Will's old sword, the one he had discarded, and Brooke had another one in his hand.

Three things: no one else seemed to be in sight. "Don't make this more complicated than it is," he said.

"Sir! What is the meaning of this?" I stamped my foot. As for Will's old sword that Brooke had thrown to me, I held it away from my body, as if it might bite.

"That pretty trick won't work," he said. "You caught that sword like a man. Now use it like one."

I had no choice. He came at me with a conventional direct attack, and I replied. The empty side street rang with the clatter of our blades. But what was he after? His mincing moves did not seem designed to kill me.

"Are you so desperate," I asked in ragged phrases, "that you must resort to meeting women in this fashion, sir?"

"You can stop pretending, Luke. I know who you are. I've followed you since you left the theater."

"Whoever I am," I shouted, surprising him with a sudden lunge, "what do you want with me?"

"I thought it would be great sport to fence with one of your kind, especially outside the presence of your erstwhile protector. Then, after our match, I'll see what you look like under those skirts." His eyebrows rose in a leer. "What you really look like."

"What do you mean, one of your kind?"

I stumbled on a cobblestone and had to parry with one knee on the ground. How could I possibly fight in fourteen yards of green gabardine? Amazingly, Brooke stepped back, giving me time to lurch to my feet.

"Your deformity would explain why Sally preferred you to me," he went on, nicking my sleeve with a neat thrust. "She was always fond of novelty."

"My deformity? What in the devil are you talking about?" My quick riposte tore a bit of lace from his collar.

"Ha! Even your salty language proves my point. That you're one of those...now, what did she call 'em? Oh, yes." His eyes lit up. "*Androgenee*. That's what you are. Both male and female at the same time."

"What? What nonsense!" I managed to drive him against the brick wall, but I stepped on my dress hem, nearly falling, and he pivoted away. Blast this dress!

"So you deny it? Ha! She said you would."

"Who said that? Sally?"

"Sally never spoke of you. It was Ellen who told me all about you and your kind. I recognized you today when

163

you were onstage costumed as a boy, and Ellen told me that you were Sally's last lover. I like novelty myself." A grimace crossed his pretty face. "And I confess that I miss the girl. Ellen hinted that you killed Sally, but you don't seem hard enough for that."

"Please. Don't flatter me. I would've bet that you killed her, Brooke." I lashed out with Will's sword, and now Brooke's cheek was no longer perfect.

Slapping at the jagged cut, he set his shoulders toward me.

"We've talked too much. Now I'd like to see who's right, you or Ellen. The time has come to see what you've got hidden."

He began his final attack, lunging at me sideways with his sword dancing at the end of his arm. His pretty face glowed with triumph. His red tongue darted from his mouth as he licked his lips in anticipation.

Instead of despair, a cold anger swept over me. Smugness in a man always has that effect. The lout drove me back, toward an alley. My body and my sword reacted defensively, just as Thomas taught me, but my mind did not retreat an inch. What did it matter that Brooke was twice as big as I? What did it matter that my dress hindered my movements? What did it matter that he might soon throw me down and lift these damned skirts and...

Recalm! The name came to me out of the blue. Recalm's strategy: "Every weakness has a hidden strength." Of course! My skirts were my weakness, but they also held an advantage. Brooke could not see my legs, could not guess what they would do, which way they would move, or how they might kick! I laughed aloud.

At the sound, Brooke eyed me quizzically and closed in for his final lunge. I held my ground one last second, another half an instant, one more breath. Then I shot my right leg straight up, catching his sword in my skirts. He jerked his hand away but too late. I flung my foot to the right, and the sword clanked against the building across the street.

Fear widened his eyes, and I drove in for the kill. The tip of my sword touched his nose. He shrank away from me, falling on the sharp bricks of the wall behind him, sliding down to the hard, stony street.

"The tide has turned, Mr. Brooke."

I kept my body as far from his hands and feet as possible, the length of my sword, though he seemed too stunned to strike out, even if he'd had a weapon.

"You will not have the pleasure of unmasking me, sir, but I will divulge a secret. Being both male and female, I carry the best and worst of each sex."

I let the sword travel down below his waist. He groaned as my sword drew a circle, as if around a target.

"At his worst," I said, "a man will kill another. At her best, a woman will show mercy. I will cut you," I went on, jabbing at his codpiece, and he groaned once more. "I will cut you some mercy, Mr. Brooke, but you must never come at me again. As far as you are concerned, I do not exist. Never speak to me, never speak of me, or next time,

I'll behave like a woman at her worst." I jabbed harder this time. "What is your answer?"

"Yes," he whispered. "Yes." Tears ran down his cheek into the lightning-shaped cut.

I stepped back, drained. Acting in an unfinished play was one thing, but writing it as I went along was exhausting.

Keeping my gaze on Brooke, I moved across the street. Slowly, I bent down, picked up his sword and backed away. His eyes did not stray from my sword hand. Turning the corner, I let my shoulders sag a bit. I did not think he would follow me. Except for the cut to his cheek, I had not hurt him. And besides (Vanity, thy name is man!), his codpiece was very well padded. But blast him! Now I would have to re-do my hair for Lord Wotton's dinner party, and my dress was ruined. I surveyed the holes in the skirt and on my sleeve.

A man and woman passed by just then, staring at the swords I carried, one in each hand. Let them stare. I was a rare breed. I was an *Androgenee*.

That reminded me. I owed Ellen a payback. A big one.

As for the swords, they were easy to dispose of. No one saw me enter our house. The back staircase is very secluded, and I had ample time to hide them under my bed before changing my dress.

I was coming down the central staircase to wait for Father when I saw a servant hurrying to the front entrance. He entered the vestibule and passed out of my sight. The instant he opened the door, I heard a familiar voice, and my spirits sank.

166

"I need to see Lord Culpeper."

I pressed my back against the corner of the landing. As eager as I was to know what message the letter contained, I was in no mood to see Henry again so soon. Perhaps I could get the servant to tell him that I...

Wait! Henry had not asked to see me.

"Yes, sir," the servant said. "May I say who is calling?"

"Lord Winter. Tell him it's urgent," he said and then added in a whisper, "tell him it's about a message I've come across."

I ran down the stairs, nearly tripping over the lace at my hem. Henry's flat black eyes tracked my descent.

"I'll speak to Lord Winter," I told the servant as I walked up. "You won't need to disturb Father."

"My dear Lucinda, you look lovely in blue." Henry took my hand, fondling the fingers before he bent to kiss my knuckles. "I'm very glad to see you again, of course, but I do need to speak to Lord Edward. Desperately, I might add."

I raised my eyebrows. His voice now had a different quality, a third note.

"Father is dressing for dinner." Though I was loath to touch Henry, I moved closer and put my lips to his ear. "Is it about the paper I gave you?"

He turned to face me, and his eyes traveled to my bosom. I had forgotten the new dress. It was rather low-cut and I felt myself blush.

167

"It's a dangerous message," Henry said, his mustache twitching. "Where did you find it, Lucinda?"

"You managed to decode it quickly," I countered, unwilling to betray my hand. "Then you must have figured out the meaning of *The Bazile?*"

"Shh!" He put his finger to his lips and pulled me into a nearby parlor. Taking the letter from his pocket, he unfolded it and pointed to those words. "Say that backwards," he whispered, watching my face.

"E-l-i-z-a-" I met his eyes, as if astounded. "*Elizabeth!*"

"Shh! Very nearly. It's an almost-perfect, backward-running anagram." Even his whisper betrayed a trace of admiration for the cryptic note. "The message tells of a plot to kill the Queen. It ends in mid-sentence, so it may continue on another page. Here's my decoded version, though it's not quite complete."

24	24
The Bazile never slumbers. Very soon	Elizabeth is ever alert. Very soon she
the creature will sleep with the dead.	will die. The plan is to come at her from
The hope of the future will shoot forth	a trash heap. It will take place on the
from amidst the offal. Mark the Eve—	Eve

I read it quickly. Henry's "translation" revealed no names except for the Queen's, but I did not need a signature to know that Lord Wotton was responsible for this. After all, I'd found it in his servant's handbag, and Sally had

168

often done errands for his lordship. Had she been a courier of treasonous materials? I held the two versions side by side.

"What does this mean about a trash heap?" I asked. "And this part at the very end? 'Mark the Eve'? Or as you said, 'It will take place on the Eve?'"

"That was the part I couldn't quite figure out since it was cut off," he said defensively. "That's why I must see your father. The plot appears to be well under way, and it may be connected to a trail he's had me working on, one that leads from Marshalsea Prison to a brothel and possibly to a theater."

I stared at the translation for a moment, pretending to read it again. If Henry told Father about this, Father would demand to know where he had gotten it, and Henry would tell him, and then all would be lost, including my acting career.

I carefully folded the two sheets together, three times over, and slipped them into my bosom. Henry's eyes followed my movements.

"Father doesn't feel well, Henry. He has to go out tonight, and he stressed that he did not want to be disturbed until it's time to go."

The lie came easily. After all, I told myself, it wasn't as if the assassination would take place tonight.

"Will you trust me to give this to him, Henry, along with your message?" I raised one shoulder and sighed.

"I suppose I could," he said. "I mean, you are his daughter. Actually, I have an engagement myself." Then he glanced away, seemed to have a change of heart and turned his cold stare on me once more. "You know how important this is, Lucinda. You do promise to give it to him, along with my translation, as soon as you see him?"

"Oh, yes, Henry. I promise. The moment I see him."

He departed, his eyes still on the pages I had promised to give Father.

CHAPTER 8
MARK THE EVE

I felt Father's eyes on me as he helped me alight from the carriage. Gazing demurely at the steps leading to Lord Wotton's home, I pulled my cloak close around my throat.

"Are you cold, Lucinda?" Father asked.

"Only a little," I said softly and glanced past his left ear.

The trick, I had determined, was to focus on something next to him. So far, it was working. So far, I had not seen Father. The moment I did see him, I would have to show him the message and Henry's translation, as I had promised. By that time, though, I hoped to have incontrovertible proof that Lord Wotton was the mastermind behind the plot to kill the Queen. Perhaps if I could pull that off, Father might begin to perceive me as something more than a porcelain doll.

Father knocked and a servant opened the door at once. I smiled to myself and walked across the threshold. Somewhere in this house, most likely in the library, was my incontrovertible proof. And I had all evening to find it. I even had the glimmer of a plan: to find a letter or note in Lord Wotton's handwriting. With that, Henry could determine if his lordship also wrote the note about The Bazile. I recalled the list of names Lord Wotton gave me for place cards, but he'd dashed those off too hastily for comparison, using the modern, Italian style, which is much quicker, and not the mixed style of the note.

In the foyer a second servant took my cloak, and a third man led Father and me down a wide corridor to the banquet hall. This part of Lord Wotton's home may have been sumptuous, but I took no notice. I was listening to Father just then and thinking about my first move. Surely, I told myself, I could find my way from the banquet hall to the library?

"The more I've thought about it," Father was saying, "the more I believe that you would like the man."

"Lord Wotton?"

"Perhaps we can sit near him at dinner."

"Oh, no, Father. We have to sit where they've put our place cards."

"Is that right?" he asked, in a tone I found condescending.

"I've heard that's how they do it at dinner parties."

"At any rate," he continued, "I'll look for Charles and make the introductions. I certainly want him to see you tonight. After that, we'll find time to mingle."

"Yes, Father."

Quickly, walking beside him, I took a lace handkerchief from my pocket and draped it as decorously as possible where the satin of my bodice was too skimpy. On no account did I wish for Lord Wotton to regard me as marriageable.

Just before we stepped into the banquet hall, I glanced down the corridor to my right and spied an open door about twenty feet away. The library? Father tugged gently on my arm, but, craning my neck, I did catch a glimpse of a tall bookshelf, just inside the door.

The banquet hall was immense, though not as large as the one we have at Tintabeney. Even Greenwich Palace did not have a hall as big as Tintabeney's. In the center of this room, two long tables were set for at least a hundred people.

We walked down three broad steps, which were flanked on either side by marble pillars and huge, potted trees. Torches set into the walls and candelabra on each table gave the illusion of daylight. Across the room, near a window, musicians were playing, violin and harpsichord, I think, though they were not visible through the crowd. Everywhere, guests laughed and talked. Several were already enjoying the bounty of Lord Wotton's wine cellar.

At least one man enjoyed it too much. I heard a raucous laugh just before someone slammed into me from behind.

"Blast!" a deep voice exclaimed. Even before I turned around, I knew it was Stephen Brooke.

"I beg your pardon, sir," Father said, pulling me closer.

Recognition was instantaneous, and in a flash Brooke's nervous smile changed to an expression of dread. His rosy cheeks faded to chalk. Almost as quickly, his hand flew to the blood-encrusted cut on one of those white cheeks.

"Very, very sorry," he said, backing away, and disappeared into a throng, his panic-stricken eyes still locked on mine.

"Are you all right, Lucinda?" Father asked, as he led us on our way again, his arm around my shoulder. In a few moments, we had woven our way to the hearth along the far wall. There, we found a blazing fire, several noblemen I was acquainted with, and Lord Charles Wotton. For my own part, I would not have disturbed the group. They were all laughing and seemed content. Father brought us to a stop directly in front of Lord Wotton. The sharp, hawk's eyes turned our way, lighting on me first. I held my breath, but they moved on to study Father and softened in a smile.

"Well, Edward, it's been a long time. Glad you came tonight." His words were slightly slurred, but I knew that he was pretending to be drunk. A man planning to assassinate the Queen would not cloud his senses.

"Thank you for inviting us, Charles. Good evening, gentlemen," Father said, nodding curtly at the group of men. "I'd like to present my daughter, Lucinda." He gently pushed me forward. "I might add that Lucinda is a quite accomplished young woman, Charles. She plays the harpsichord and reads and writes in several languages."

If the earth had opened up just then, I would gladly have leaped into the chasm. Why hadn't Father simply draped a sign around my neck? *Marriageable daughter, dowry negotiable.*

"I, uh, I'm delighted to meet your charming daughter." Lord Wotton bowed and turned to his companions. "Gentlemen, do all of you know Lady Belinda?"

"Lucinda," I said at once.

"Of course, of course. Please excuse me."

174

He took a quick sip and smiled at me through clenched teeth. We passed several more minutes together, equally as scintillating. Finally, as even hell must, I suppose, it came to an end. Vague pleasantries were said all around, and we moved on.

"I do believe," Father whispered to me after we had gone a little distance away, "I do believe, Lucinda, that you made a good impression on Lord Charles."

"Whatever you say, Father."

Even a spy can be blind where his daughter is concerned.

Soon Father paused to greet someone he knew, and I scanned the room for a familiar face to use as a pretext for escape.

"Good to see you, too, Peter," Father said, and we were on our way again.

"Who was that gentleman?" I asked, merely to be polite.

"I doubt you've heard of him. A fellow named Peter Street."

I halted and whirled around, coming dangerously close to actually looking at Father just then. "Peter Street is a man, not a road?"

"Peter Street is a very wealthy tradesman. He owns warehouses near the river. Oh, and I understand he has a boathouse where the Queen keeps her barge. Typical tradesman type." Father waved his hand as if dismissing him. "I do think he's too old for you, Lucinda. Besides which, he is married."

"Father dear," I said sweetly, "why don't we separate for a while? Just until dinner? There's Ann Woolfolk near the door. I'll speak to her and meet you at the table."

I fled before he could refuse.

Hurrying to the entrance (but not in Ann Woolfolk's direction), I sank against the back of a pillar. Close by, a potted tree concealed me and my full skirt from all but the gray tabby who had evidently escaped from Alice's kitchen. In exchange for his silence, I allowed him access to the ribbons at my hem. Finally, I had a moment to think in earnest.

"Peter Street!" I whispered. The name on the card from Sally's handbag was a man and not a road! But what about the number 24 on the message? Could that be the number of the boathouse where the Queen moored her barge? "The barge!" I said aloud. Will and I had sat on the wharf, and I had peered down at a boathouse below. Could the faded letters in front of the word "Street" have once spelled out the name Peter and the number 24?

Voices nearby roused me. Peering through the branches of the potted tree, I found myself just a foot away from a scolding Ellen Beddoes.

"We've been here only half an hour," she was saying, "and you're already drunk."

"Am not." Gilbert Dereham's large frame swayed uneasily, like a galleon on a swelling sea.

I squinted through the leaves of the tree. My word! Lord Wotton must've invited half his guests this afternoon. I had written no cards for these people.

"Don't be so quick to deny it," Ellen said with a hard smile. "Drunkenness is your best virtue."

"And a tart tongue is yours," Gilbert replied, falling into a chair at the base of the tree.

"You've never had the pleasure of my tongue." She looked down at him with disdain. She was dressed more richly than I had ever seen her, with lace touching every place her skin was exposed. A good deal of lace, in other words.

"Sally's tongue wasn't half so tart."

"What do you know about Sally?" Ellen asked, perching on the arm of the chair next to Gilbert's. "She hardly ever spoke to you."

"True. True," he said with a deep sigh. "But I do miss the girl for her pretty face. What could possess a man to kill such a beautiful creature?"

"How do you know it was a man?"

"Ha! Was it you then?" Gilbert gave a silly laugh.

"Murder requires some kind of passion," Ellen said, tossing her blond curls. "I didn't feel anything at all for Sally."

"What about your precious Thomas? Didn't Sally take 'im away from you?"

"Thomas was becoming a bore."

She glanced down at her hand and ran her thumb across the fingertips. I thought it a casual gesture till I saw the red-crusted, pin-pricks on the white skin.

"Besides," she went on with a secret smile, "Thomas never appreciated what I did for him, all my sacrifices. I need a man who appreciates me for what I am."

For the past minute, a remote region of my mind's eye had followed a vaguely familiar passerby, a hunch-backed, bespectacled graybeard in velvets and silks who seemed to be hovering over Ellen's shoulder, as if trying to do what I was doing, but without benefit of proper cover. Finally, when his glasses slid off his nose, I saw through his disguise. It was my cousin Thomas. The heavy beard concealed his bruises, and a jeweled hat cast a shadow over his swollen eyes. Abruptly, he laughed to himself and vanished quickly into the noisy throng.

Ellen drew a sudden, deep breath, the lace at her bosom rippling. "Gilbert!" she whispered loudly. "Who's that fellow coming in now? The one with the thin mustache?"

"No idea," Gilbert answered without looking up. His head began to nod. Hearing footsteps at my back, I slid farther behind the pillar and the potted tree. The cat, tiring of my ribbons, darted away straight under the feet of the newcomer, Henry Rendle, young Lord Winter.

My word, again! So *this* was Henry's engagement.

Just then, Henry's booted foot connected with the cat's midsection and sent it flying.

"I...don't...like...cats!" Henry said, hardly moving his lips.

The yelping cat tore out of the banquet hall and down the corridor. Several people threw angry looks at Henry, but Ellen's reaction was uniquely Ellen's.

"Neither do I," she said, her eyes glittering. She approached Henry and put her hand on his arm. "My name is Ellen Beddoes. And you are..."

"Henry Rendle," he said, unable to take his eyes from her exuberant bosom.

A servant passed by with a tray of drinks, and Ellen took two of them while knocking over a third. She and Henry were soon lost in conversation.

And my heart leaped with joy at my sweet revenge. Never have any two creatures deserved each other more. I wanted to dance, but I thought it best to temper my enthusiasm. Other things were happening.

Less than three feet to the left of my potted tree, and probably too far away for Ellen or Henry to hear, servants were setting a table with glasses and wine bottles.

"Now, boys," I heard one of them say in a low voice, "you got to be ready at the signal."

I peered around the pillar and saw Basset's impassive face. Standing at his side and listening raptly to every word were two young men, and I knew one of them at once: my swordsman of yesterday, the murder-minded Patrick. I shook my head, disbelieving my eyes. After the wound I gave him last night, Patrick should not be able to stand at all, but stand, he did. His blue eyes suddenly narrowed in a frown. "I thought we'd have to wait for the scraps from the dinner table."

"The wagon's already piled high with scraps from the kitchen," Basset answered in a soft voice.

The other servant, a man I had never seen before, laughed softly. "Dumping in the Thames isn't exactly legal, but neither is the other thing we're planning to do."

Patrick rubbed his hands together and leaned in close to whisper. "It looks as if we'll finish up this *rosemary* business tonight, once and for all."

"Watch your tongue, man." Basset scowled, and Patrick shrank back. "The walls have ears."

"No one's listen..."

Basset stepped closer, and Patrick clamped his lips shut. "As I said, watch your tongue or I'll cut it out. You're a fool, Toby, just like your brothers, and if they weren't such fools, they'd be going with us, instead of waiting in the servants' quarters. Those two had a simple killing to pull off last night, but they nearly got killed themselves."

The one he had called Toby, the one I had thought was Patrick, and he hung his head. "They said there was two of 'em, and the second one jist came out of nowhere, like a madman."

Basset dismissed his words with a sneer.

What are they talking about, I wondered. *Last night's attack on Thomas? Could this man who looked like Patrick be his brother?* That was what Basset had seemed to imply, and Basset had called him *Toby.* My brain felt slow and heavy as the solution finally registered: Toby was a twin to Patrick. That would explain why he was able to stand on a leg that I was positive I had injured. That would explain why he had not seemed to recognize me in the kitchen yesterday afternoon. But, and this was the most

180

puzzling question: why had Basset ordered Thomas to be killed? My eavesdropping had proved one thing, however; Basset certainly knew about the *rosemary* business.

"Like I said," Basset went on. "Just wait for the signal."

A bell rang then, and everyone in the hall turned toward the sound. Lord Wotton stood in the center of the room beside a servant holding a shiny, silver bell. A chill ran down my spine. Was this the signal Basset meant?

"Before we move to the table for dinner," Lord Wotton said with a broad smile, "I'd like to propose a toast." He gripped the back of a chair with one hand and held his wine glass high with the other. All around the room, others joined him. Basset and Toby moved through the crowd with the other servants, carrying trays full of glasses for those guests caught unprepared. If the bell had been the signal, I wondered, then why were Basset and the other servants still here? Lord Wotton stood quietly until all his guests held wine glasses.

"To the kindest and wisest of her sex," he began, lifting his glass even higher. "To the most gracious of women,"

I thought I knew where he was headed with this and wondered idly how his guests would react when he toasted a woman who'd been dead for a year.

"May she live long and well," he went on, making one word of the last three. "To the pearl of England...to our most benevolent monarch...to Queen Elizabeth."

"Hear! Hear!" A chorus of men cried out in agreement.

The room grew silent while glasses were turned upside down. Now I didn't know what to think about Lord Wotton. Perhaps I had been so much in the company of actors that I could not recognize sincerity.

"I'll drink to that," Stephen Brooke said. He had walked up beside Ellen, and now he grabbed a drink from a servant's tray, draining it in one gulp.

"You look awful," Ellen said. "What happened to your face?"

"None o' your concern!" he snapped. "Except that it's all your fault." Lifting another glass, he drank it, too. "All because of something you told me."

"What did I tell you?" Ellen's lip curled up in a sarcastic smile.

Brooke opened his mouth to speak, but his eyes turned cloudy. He reached for a third glass. "Never mind," he said, downing it and wiping his mouth. "I'm so addled I don't even know what day it is."

"For what it's worth," Ellen said with a world-weary sigh, "it's the twenty-fourth."

"April the twenty-fourth," Gilbert said, lifting his head from his chest. His voice was as thick as yesterday's gravy.

Everyone turned to him, startled. Henry seemed astonished the man was there.

"Go back to sleep, Gilbert," Ellen said, rolling her eyes.

"Today is St. Mark's Eve," Gilbert went on, slurring his words as if he spoke out of a deep sleep. Just then Basset passed by with a tray of drinks. Gilbert raised his hand

and took a glass from the tray. "Thank you, my good man." Draining the glass in one gulp, he placed it on the edge of Basset's tray and hiccupped loudly. His hand waved limply in the air. "You may go," he said as his head fell forward onto his chest.

"Listen to his lordship, would you?" Brooke said, rolling his eyes at Ellen. She obliged him with a laugh.

Henry did not laugh. Nor did I. I almost cried out in shock.

"Today is St. Mark's Eve," Gilbert had said. Mark the Eve. The last words of the cryptic message. Number 24 for April twenty-fourth. This very night the Queen was to be killed, but because of me, Father knew nothing of the plot. The plan, Henry's version had said, is to come at her from a trash heap. Basset had spoken of trash, table scraps from tonight's dinner, and he had talked of dumping trash in the Thames. I had to tell Father, and at once.

I stepped away from the pillar toward Henry and promptly froze. Within arm's reach, but with their backs turned, were Basset and Toby, the servant I had thought was Patrick. I cast my eyes down, fumbled with the lace at my wrist and tried not to breathe. If they should recognize me...

"Blast, man!" Basset's voice was a harsh whisper. "Didn't you hear me? It's time to go."

Toby stood his ground. "But I just saw one of them fellows that was in the kitchen yesterday."

My scalp tightened. I dared not even lift my head to look for Father.

"The one you did not see," Toby added, "the one that gibbered some nonsense about Sally's shoemaker."

I jerked my head up sharply.

"He was snoopin' around, and then he slipped into the library," Toby finished.

Basset nodded. "You tell the others it's time and then go on to the kitchen. I'll take care of that fellow in the library. If I don't, his snoopin' will interfere with our plans." He snickered. "Dead men don't do much snoopin', do they?"

Toby laughed, and I must have gasped aloud. Basset turned to glare at me, and my hand flew to my neck.

"Good evenin', miss," he said evenly.

My cold fingers gripped my throat, making speech impossible.

"Would you care for some wine, miss?" He lifted a glass from the tray he held.

I brought it to my lips and held his gaze. Up close, I saw the makeup on the bruise around his eye. He bowed and then disappeared among the guests in the banquet hall. With my hand trembling, I drained the glass and dropped it at the trunk of the potted tree.

As I approached the little group, Brooke took one look at me, blanched and fled in the opposite direction. Henry stood as before, except now he was rubbing his forehead. When I touched his arm, he jumped, and Ellen glowered at me.

"Henry, I must return something to you," I said. "And make a confession."

"Confession?" Ellen's blue eyes narrowed. "You were that little actor in the play. What are you doing here?"

"Trying to keep up with the rumors you start about me, Ellen." I turned so that she could see my movements, and then I pulled the folded pages from my bosom and put them into Henry's hand. The lace handkerchief slipped to one side, but it did not concern me now. "You must see to this message," I said gravely. "I have spoken of it to no one.

This last was a lie. I had told Will, and now Will was in peril.

Henry's eyebrows shot up. "Lord Edward doesn't know?"

I shook my head. "Father needs to hear this news from you. You're his assistant. Besides, I have something more important to do."

"More important than saving the..." He stopped himself just in time. "I must find Lord Edward."

"There," I said and pointed to Father across the room.

Then Henry strode off to save the Queen.

I had a mission also and turned away, nearly tripping on the torn ribbons at my hem.

My dress! I had forgotten. Will would not recognize me in this dress.

It did not matter. Nothing else mattered. Somehow, I had to reach Will before Basset did. My pulse racing, I darted into the hallway, leaving the party behind.

I ran down the empty hall and came to a breathless stop at the library door. It was closed, yet when Father and I had entered the house, this door was open. My hand shook as I gripped the cold, metal latch.

I slipped inside, closing the door behind me, and saw that I was alone. A chill ran up my bare arms. The room had looked so different in the morning sunlight. Now, candles threw dancing shadows on the walls, even to the top of the domed ceiling. Dark curtains covered the windows, and Lady Sophie's face glared at me from her portrait. The weight of all the things I did not know settled on my shoulders like a mantle of gloom.

I did not know who had killed Sally.

I did not know how to prevent the death of the Queen.

I did not know where Will might be.

My eyes fell on the ottoman that I had seen Basset open. Was that only this morning, I asked myself as I hurried to the low stool. The fabric covering was luxurious and thick to my touch, with a pattern of dark red roses which I had not been able to see when I had looked in the window. Slowly, I lifted the ottoman lid but instantly dropped it back in place. A noise at the door made me stand up straight and turn around. "Will?" I said softly to myself, only to whisper, "Basset?" in the next moment.

Then I did exactly what Will had done. I bolted toward the tapestry on the side wall. When the door finally creaked open, I was standing in the darkness, breathing rapidly but hidden from sight, I hoped. My dress, with most of the skirt stuffed behind me, had squeezed reluctantly into the small space. Footsteps echoed in the room, and I forgot the dress and squinted through the numerous little holes in the tapestry. A shadow moved on the opposite wall, and a figure appeared in the center of the room. A man, surely, but who? My eyes, not yet adjusted to the dark, saw nothing clearly. The figure halted in the center of the room, bent low over the ottoman and lifted up the lid. When he stood up again, a smile on his roguish face, I smiled, too and opened my mouth to call out. Only then did my dilemma occur to me. Who should I say I was? I drew my breath in sharply, the tiniest of sounds, yet he heard me. Those dark eyes cut toward the tapestry. Drawing his sword, he advanced on my hiding place. "Will," I said softly. "No!"

He halted. "Who calls my name?"

"It's me," I said, still uncertain which me to be.

"The voice is Luke's," he said, his eye traveling down the tapestry, "but not the shoes."

"Oh, blast!" I whispered, touching my bodice to make sure the handkerchief was still there. To my horror, I realized it was *not* at the same moment that Will lifted the arras. And just like that, I knew what role to play. As so often happens in life, my costume gave me the cue.

"That's because..." I answered, meeting his gaze, "because I am not Luke." He cocked his head. His hand was still on his sword. "My name is Lucy," I went on. "I am Luke's sister. His twin sister."

"Indeed?" His eyes swept down my frame, lingered over certain aspects, and came full circle back to my face. "May I say then, milady, that eccentricity is a powerful force in your family. Nevertheless, I am pleased to make your acquaintance. William H. Shakespeare, at your service," he said, making a small half-bow.

I burst from the niche, smoothing my skirt down as I moved.

"I already know who you are," I said, turning to face him. "Luke told me all about you. We tell each other everything."

"How intriguing. Lucy, did you say? I suppose that's why you knew about the niche behind the arras, then?"

"Yes," I said, and his gaze was so straightforward that I almost stopped right there. His dark eyes that always saw through to the heart of a matter nearly made me give up all my attempts at pretense. *Is he even now,* I wondered, *analyzing the way I play this role? And which role does he think I am playing?* All this went through my mind, but I had come too far to turn back now. And lies came so easily. "Luke could not be here tonight," I said. "Father sent him on a special mission. I came to warn you, but a noise frightened me into hiding," I finished.

"Warn me of what?" he asked

"Basset is on his way here to kill you. I overheard him talking with some servants. I think he's the mastermind behind the plot to kill the Queen. He's the one who sent

188

Jack and Patrick to attack Thomas last night. And they have a brother, the man you and Luke met here in the kitchen yesterday. Luke thought the fellow was Patrick, but he's Patrick's twin."

"Another set of twins?" Will broke in with a quick laugh. "And Taverner told me that I shouldn't use two sets in my play. *Overcooked coincidence*, he called it."

"Forget your play," I snapped. "The assassination is set for tonight, very soon, I think. Basset told the men to wait for his signal, but now it's time. Toby only whispered the word *rosemary*, and Basset threatened to cut out his tongue. They've got a wagon in the alley, piled high with garbage. They plan to dump the garbage into the Thames as an excuse to drive the wagon to the wharf. The Queen will be on the river, on her royal barge, and they'll be ready. I don't know how, muskets perhaps, but they definitely plan to kill the Queen. 'The hope of the future,' the note said, 'will shoot forth from amidst the offal.' And there's the rest of the note, the words, 'Mark the Eve.' I only figured that part out a few minutes ago. In the banquet hall, Gilbert Dereham, drunk as he was, announced that today is St. Mark's Eve. The twenty-fourth of April is the Eve of St. Mark. Today, Will, is when they plan to kill the Queen. Tonight."

I jerked my head toward the door. "But I almost forgot why I came. Basset is on his way to the library. Patrick's twin saw you come in here."

"I hoped as much. I've been entering and exiting this room quite often in the past quarter hour just to attract attention."

I turned sharply to stare at him.

He grinned. "I guess that proves I know how to stage an entrance, doesn't it?"

"You wanted him to see you? But your children? I mean, Luke told me what you said. You couldn't risk..."

"I figured out that cryptic note, also, and I recalled an oath I made before the age of twenty. Perhaps your young men don't have the same custom here in London, but I, along with all my Stratford school mates, swore fealty to Her Majesty even at the risk of our own lives."

He stared at my dress then, as if seeing it for the first time, and my hand involuntarily went to my bosom.

"I thank you, Lucy," he said, "for risking your life to warn me, but you won't be any help when Basset comes. In fact, you will be in great danger yourself, and you'll make my job more difficult." He lifted the tapestry.

"Please, step inside."

I realized that he was right. For the first time since I had met him, I did what he said without arguing. He let the tapestry fall, and darkness swallowed me up again, but only for an instant. The very next moment I heard the library door open. Whoever it was, I realized, must be holding a candelabrum, because a multitude of shadows flared up on the opposite wall. I heard the sound of an object being set down, the shadows stilled and the room was suddenly much brighter. "Well, good evenin'," a man's voice said, and I knew that it was Basset.

Will stepped away from Lord Wotton's high-backed chair, came to a halt near the ottoman and bowed in Basset's direction. I could see only Will's profile. His hands seemed to be clasped at his back, but I fervently hoped he held a sword.

"And a good evening to you, too," Will said. "Basset," he added.

There was silence for a moment. "Beg pardon," Basset finally said. "Have we met?"

"No. But it was in this room that I first saw you, Basset, that I first laid eyes on your toad-spotted self."

Will practically spit out the word that Londoners reserve for traitors. I could not see Basset, but he must have stood there in great confusion. Will spoke like a nobleman, and he had a nobleman's bearing, yet Basset knew that he had never met this man in Lord Wotton's library.

"Now surely, sir," Basset said, in the syrupy tone he had used to placate Lord Wotton, "surely you're mistaken. Might it be you've had too much to drink? Perhaps I should escort you back to the banquet hall. You are one of his lordship's guests, aren't you?"

"Actually, I've never met his lordship, either, but I have seen the man, also in this room, and with your toadying self, bowing and scraping to him."

I now saw Basset for the first time, as he began making his way slowly toward Will. He had the look of a cat confident of a cornered mouse.

"And what might you a' been doin' in Lord Wotton's library, sir? If you don't mind my askin'. Did you find a bottle of 'is lordship's wine, by any chance?"

"What does one do in a library, Basset?" Will's voice was edged with steel. "I was reading."

He held up a green-tinged pamphlet, *Leicester's Commonwealth*. I stifled a cry, and Basset halted in his tracks.

"This seems uncommon peculiar behavior, sir." Basset folded his arms and cocked his head at Will. "I should take you back to the party, I'm sure of it."

"Oh, I'm not going to the party," Will said, flipping the pamphlet open with one hand. "And neither are you."

Basset resumed his advance, though more warily now. "If you be the same fellow Toby warned me about, he told me you spoke a lot of nonsense."

"Oh, but none of it is nonsense," Will said, raising the pamphlet for emphasis. "You shall not return to Lord Wotton's party, and I have been in this room before. Yesterday afternoon, for instance, I was admiring his lordship's fine library when I suddenly stumbled over the ottoman, and this pamphlet fell onto the floor. I returned it to its hiding place, of course."

"But of course," Basset said, the condescension returning to his voice as he drew nearer. "And tonight, you jist decided to come back for it, I s'pose."

"Then you have supposed wrong, Basset." Will tossed *Leicester's Commonwealth* aside, without taking his eyes from the man. "Actually, I came back for the pamphlet this morning. I planned to pass that little book on to a friend, one who has connections with the Queen's spy ministry. But no sooner had I entered the room, than Lord Wotton appeared at the door, and I was obliged to take refuge. Moments later, you appeared. It was when his lordship left to change his shirt that you did a most bizarre thing."

Basset gave a cheerless laugh and halted again, two long strides from Will. "Change his shirt?" he repeated slowly. "And what was it you seen me do?"

"You spoke...to a piece of furniture. You lifted the top of the ottoman and addressed a soliloquy to its contents."

Basset shook his head, genuinely startled. "And how..."

Will brought his other hand from behind his back. In the candlelight, the blade of a sword made a shining arc, before the sharp point came to rest on Basset's breastbone.

"Have a seat," Will said, "until a friend of mine arrives. Oh, by the way, the assassination scheduled for tonight has been canceled."

Basset's wide eyes never left Will's face as the sword prodded him backward in the direction of Lord Wotton's chair. His boots collided with the ottoman, and he stumbled, just as Will had done. Basset came up, not with a pamphlet, but with a sword, the same one I'd noticed yesterday, lying on a bookshelf.

Blade met blade, and the fight was on.

"Best hope your friend comes quick," Basset snarled.

CHAPTER 9
GOODNIGHT, MR. SHAKESPEARE

Basset's unexpected discovery of a sword for himself was creating havoc in Lord Wotton's library, and I was powerless to help Will. They managed to knock over a table filled with books, upend Lord Wotton's chair and slam into the wall where I hid behind the tapestry. The brick-shaped Basset was taller and bigger, and Will's actions were merely responses to each broadsided attack. My eyes roved the room, desperate to find some way to help Will, some way to keep him from being killed. I was no more help than old Homer, whose bust stared sightlessly from the shelf beside the window. When I saw a sword glimmering on the nearest wall, my spirits soared. *I can help,* I thought, *dress or no dress.* My fingers were taking hold of the rough backside of the tapestry, when the door opened noisily. I froze. Basset's eyes flicked toward the door. Immediately, Will struck him high on the shoulder, drawing blood. Basset retreated, slapping at the wound, and I saw Thomas, still in disguise, hurry toward the two men, whipping his sword from its sheath.

"I came as soon as I got your note," he said. "I say there, Will, wouldn't you like some help?"

Once more Basset looked away. Perhaps Thomas's words had unnerved him. Will's blade whistled high on his cheek. Blood trickled from the cut, and Basset's counterattack lacked any hint of strategy.

"Thanks for the offer," Will said, keeping his eyes on his opponent, "but I think I can manage. Take a seat, if you like."

A circular rug covered the floor in the center of the room, and the two men prowled its outer edge. Basset scowled at Will, seeming to take his measure more carefully now. Thomas moved to a chair against the far wall and dropped into it, laying his sword on the floor beside him and pulling a slip of paper from his pocket.

"When Alice handed me your note," he said, "I was quite busy. In fact, I was sure you were joking. But she assured me you were dead serious. What's this about a uh..." He removed his spectacles and laughed again but without humor. "A plot to, uh, to kill the Queen?"

Will did not reply, but only because he was executing a very smooth *balestra*. At the last moment, Basset sidestepped and began an attack of his own. The clang of metal on metal echoed off the domed ceiling. Sweat bathed each man's face. The makeup that had neatly covered Basset's bruised skin was now streaked and spotty.

"Sorry to interrupt." Thomas raised his hand, lines of worry etching his face. "Tell me later."

"It's no trouble," Will said. "In my line of work, as you know, I'm used to talking while I move about. But regarding that plot you mentioned, this particular servant," Will went on, combining his words with a well-timed lunge, "this Basset could answer any question you may have. For instance, Basset, would you like to tell Thomas what's in the alley?"

The question sent Basset into a greater rage. He met Will's attack like a wild man. I glimpsed his eyes and wished Will had accepted Thomas's offer to help. At the moment, Will was moving nimbly enough, but he had proved yesterday that he was not London's greatest swordsman.

I squeezed my eyes shut, but I couldn't *not* watch. My eyes flew open again. Will and Basset stood barely two feet from me, their blades locked. For a long moment, they hardly moved, as still as a frieze of gladiators. And then Will made a kind of grunting sound through clenched teeth and shoved Basset away. The two circled the fringe of the rug once more.

"I'll get back to you later, Thomas," Will said with a quick grin. "This fellow and I were having our own conversation when you entered."

"Certainly." Thomas waved his hand. "Carry on."

"As I was telling you, Basset," Will continued, so casually that one would think they'd never been interrupted, "I returned to this house to get your copy of *Leicester's Commonwealth.*"

At mention of the pamphlet, Thomas sat up straighter, and Basset rushed at Will. Their blades clanged again. In ragged phrases, Will resumed the conversation.

"You hid the pamphlet in the ottoman, didn't you? Tonight, after you had succeeded in murdering the Queen, and after your escape, you were planning to give out the rumor that Lord Wotton was in charge of the assassination plot. Finding *Leicester's Commonwealth* in Lord Wotton's library would convince the authorities of his treachery, wouldn't it?"

Basset spoke no answer except with his sword. Will countered each one expertly, gracefully. For the first time, an unpleasant possibility came to mind, that I had been deceived by this actor.

"And there's the problem of Sally. What about that girl, Basset?" Will went on, without so much as a gasp for breath. "Were you as surprised as I, to learn that Sally was a prostitute?"

Thomas moved to the edge of his seat.

"Or did you know that?" Will persisted. "Is that why you left her hanging from a tree in the Single Woman's Graveyard, a place reserved for prostitutes?"

"One shouldn't speak ill of the dead," Basset replied, barely avoiding Will's *stoccata.*

Where had Will learned to thrust under his opponent's sword and break to the left? He had done nothing like that yesterday.

"Of course," Will went on, "Sally was only your courier. She went to Marshalsea Prison for you, didn't she, Basset? She carried coded messages in a fancy handbag, one that you stole from Lady Sophie's room, I imagine."

Basset attacked just then, and Will answered with a brutal *riposte.* After a clangorous exchange, they circled the rug again.

"And then," Will went on, "Sally must've asked you for money. You complained once that no matter what Sally had, she always wanted more. Quite naturally, you felt you had to kill her. But Thomas was looking for Sally, and so you had to send Patrick and Jack to take care of him, didn't you?"

Thomas leaned forward at this news. One hand reached for his sword, but he kept his seat.

Basset attacked again, the point of his sword ripping through Will's sleeve. I squeezed my eyes shut, but only for a second. When I looked again, Will seemed unhurt.

"Twice you sent them out," Will said, "but they failed to kill Thomas, just as you are failing to kill me."

"I don't know what you're talkin' about," Basset said, breathing rapidly.

"Oh, but I think you do."

Will leaped back to avoid Basset's clumsy coup. These two squared off once more, eyeing each other's every move.

"And I think you know about that wagon in the alley," Will went on, his breath coming raggedly now. "The wagon that you and your accomplices have piled high with garbage from the kitchen—potato peelings, cabbage leaves, apple cores, but underneath, there's an oilskin cloth, and under that a load of muskets. Those muskets make no sense, unless one happens to know that the Queen will soon be out on the river, taking the evening air on her royal barge."

"The Queen?" Thomas leaped to his feet. "How do you know this?"

"I found a note in Sally's handbag. She was supposed to deliver it for Basset, but he killed her before she got a chance—killed her simply because he thought she was too greedy. He kills, by the way, in the same manner he fights. Stupidly."

Basset rushed at Will, no strategy, no subtlety, just rage.

"Stupidly," Will repeated, meeting Basset's blade with equal strength. The sound of the clash echoed painfully in my little niche. "You didn't plan that move, Basset, and you didn't plan Sally's murder. If you had, you would have looked through the girl's handbag to make sure she had delivered each copy of your cryptic message. Lord Wotton's dinner party *had* to take place tonight, didn't it? On the twenty-fourth, so that you and your band of assassins would have an excuse to drive a wagonload of garbage to the Thames."

Thomas still watched the parrying and lunging from his place beside the chair. At least there, he was out of the way. Which was more than I could say for myself. The battle was coming uncomfortably close.

The door opened. Again.

"What in the devil is going on here?" the newcomer demanded in a voice I recognized at once. My father's gray eyes scanned the room, and I involuntarily shrank back into the niche.

"Oh, hello, Uncle Edward," Thomas said, gesturing to the chair next to his. "Here, have a seat. This shouldn't take much longer."

Henry Rendle hurried into the room just behind Father. When he saw the fight and heard the clash of blades, he took a backward step, using the door as a shield.

"My word, Thomas," he said, putting only his head into the room. "How can you sit there, calmly enjoying a friendly duel? What are those two doing? Are they drunk? Get up, man! The Queen's life is in imminent danger."

The battle began to edge toward him, and Henry fled behind the door again.

"If you insist, Henry," Thomas said, laughing and getting to his feet, "then I'll stand, but there's nothing to worry about."

Henry shook his head gravely. "I think you may not know the whole situation, Thomas. I just this minute told Lord Edward of a plot..."

Thomas waved his hand for silence and moved aside to let Will and Basset pass by. "Excellent *coup de fond* there, Will! Oh, I know about the plot, Henry, but everything's under control now. Will!" he shouted. "Watch out for his—whew! Good man."

Basset tried an advancing attack, but Will parried it with an exquisite *imbrocata,* breaking perfectly to the right. I'd seen the trick in di Grassi's book, the one that Will had borrowed from Lord Wotton. *Surely,* I thought, *Will had been too busy to practice that trick.* But the evidence was mounting. Yesterday I was deceived, and damnably so.

"As I was saying, Uncle Edward," Thomas went on, keeping his eyes on the fight, "things are under control. We'll have to confiscate the muskets in the alley and round up Basset's accomplices, but the Queen's no longer in any danger."

"But we just found out about the plot," Henry moaned. "How can it be over?"

Will and Basset slammed into the bookshelves near the door, and Father took shelter with Henry. Books crashed to the floor, books that Will ordinarily might have coveted.

Thomas seemed only just now to hear Henry's question and spared him a quick glance. "For a couple of weeks," he answered, "I've been checking out some rumors from Sir Francis Walsingham's office. You'll recall, sir," he said, turning to Father, "that I dropped by your house last night to fill you in on what I'd learned so far."

More books crashed to the floor and everyone jumped, including me. Basset fought without thinking now, woodenly responding to Will's thrusts and lunges.

"About those rumors, Henry," Thomas went on, "one of them led me to this very house. A young servant girl supposedly was taking messages to known criminal elements. I befriended her, hoping to infiltrate the conspiracy. A few days ago, she was killed by this villain, Basset. Good man, Will. You're tiring him out."

As if on cue, Will brought his blade down hard on Basset's sword, just above the hilt. The sword broke apart, striking Basset on his forearm. He cried out in pain, stumbling backward across the rug, but Will pursued him, driving him to his knees.

With a last thrust of his sword, Will took aim at Basset's scalp and lifted the wavy, black locks from his head. The wig sailed off, landing at Father's feet, and Basset's hands flew up. One covered his bald head. The other waved frantically in surrender. Like the mighty Myconides whom he had played onstage, Will stood triumphant at the last.

The knave! The scoundrel!

I almost yelled the words in anger. Now I knew Will had deceived me. He let me win yesterday's sword fight. I could never forgive him. My hand flew to my heaving bosom. And his words came back to me: "I've known many a young person who assumed a disguise to keep Papa from knowing what he did." I tugged on my bodice and glared at the pirate-faced rogue. Well! I'd be hanged if I ever let him know that I was on to him.

Henry bent down to pick up the wig. "I don't believe it," he said. "That's..."

"John Maines," Father finished. "Banished from England three years ago at the Babington trials, forbidden to return, on pain of death."

Still on his knees, the man Father identified as Maines wheeled around. His face was bright red, and not just from the cut Will had inflicted on his cheek.

"Aye," he said. "Death comes to us all, even to the whoreson bitch you call your queen."

At Basset's first words, Thomas moved to the window and yanked down the drapery cords. Then, pulling Basset's arms behind his back, he trussed him up, neat as a netted fish.

"Lock me up," Basset continued, his voice rising to a shrill pitch, even as Thomas wrenched his arms. "Tear me limb from limb, but there's others will come after me. They're here already, and they'll send Anne Boleyn's bastard—rose to the hell she..."

Basset continued ranting, more enraged than ever, but not another syllable of blasphemy reached our ears, because Thomas had pulled the velvet cap off his own head, stuffed the cap into Basset's open mouth, and tied it in place with the drapery cord. After a moment, my accomplished cousin stepped away, pleased with himself.

"Nice work, Thomas," Father said. "This shows how one can be fooled, I suppose. I never would have thought Maines was clever enough to devise a plot like this. At any rate, you did a remarkable job, my boy. And who's this other fellow with the admirable swordsmanship? Your assistant, I take it?"

"Why...yes, sir. His name's..."

"The name is Lancer," Will broke in, bowing courteously. "Will Lancer, at your service, Lord Edward. I'm but a humble citizen of England and a loyal servant of Her Majesty."

Thomas, trained as an actor and a spy, did not hesitate. "I was about to tell my uncle why you and Maines were fighting, Lancer, but why don't you tell him? And while you're at it, you can tell him how you knew that Maines wore a wig."

"I found a copy of *Leicester's Commonwealth* in this room," Will said, tapping the floor with the point of his sword. "Basset had planted the pamphlet to throw suspicion onto Lord Wotton. When I confronted him with it, we began to fight. As for the wig...I've always had a knack for seeing through disguises."

"Take note of this," Father said, arching an eyebrow at Henry. "While you were busy working out the words of that cryptic note, this young...assistant was dealing with treason the proper way, with a sword." He rubbed his hands together as if everything on that subject had now been said. "Well, my boys, let's clean up this affair. Henry, find that pamphlet and bring it along. Thomas, bring this Maines fellow. You mentioned his accomplices. Where can we find them?"

Thomas glanced at Will.

"They're probably in the kitchen, Thomas," Will said quickly. "The three brothers should be easy to round up, especially Jack and Patrick, since they were wounded earlier in a sword fight. They may be in the servants' quarters. Toby is Patrick's twin and likely to be a bit more fleet of foot."

"And Lord Wotton?" Father asked. "Is he absolutely free of suspicion?"

"Oh, yes, sir, completely free of suspicion," Thomas answered with a laugh, pulling Basset to his feet. "Everyone knows that Lord Wotton loves his wine too much to spend time on politics. Now, if those were bottles of French wine in the alley, instead of muskets, then I'd assume Lord Wotton was the ringleader."

I bit my tongue to keep from crying out in anger. "Everyone knows," Thomas had said. Had my own father known about Lord Wotton's drunkenness, and yet he still paraded me in front of the man?

Father shrugged. "I'm sure you're right, Thomas. I'll make arrangements for getting Lucinda home, and then I'll find Lord Wotton and tell him what has transpired here. We owe him that at least. No sensitive details, of course, just the fact that we've taken several of his servants to the Tower."

Father paused to give Will an appraising glance. "And I'm sure there will be some kind of commendation in this for you, young fellow. Lancer, was it?"

"Yes, sir. Thank you. It has been an honor." Will bowed low.

"By the way, drop by my home tomorrow," Father added. "The ministry can use a man with your powers of deduction." He clapped his hands together dramatically. "Well, let's go, gentlemen. We still have much work ahead of us."

In rapid succession, Father led the way to the door, Thomas dragged Basset across the rug, and Henry followed, holding tightly to the green pamphlet. The door shut noisily behind them, and I waited patiently a whole minute.

"Will," I whispered, "do you think it's safe to..."

A sound made me hush. The door opened once more, and I heard footsteps and then the closing of the door.

"Thomas," Will said, "did you forget something?"

"I say, Will," Thomas began. He stepped forward, and I could see him clearly. "I wonder if you'd mind telling me how you knew I was here tonight. And how'd you know Alice would give me a note? She hunted me down in the banquet hall."

"I made her a promise," Will said, as he righted Lord Wotton's chair. "I told her that giving you the note would get Basset into deep trouble. You had happened to come into the kitchen earlier, right after I stepped out into the alley. I had left the rear door ajar, and when I heard voices, I peered around the door and saw you talking to Alice. You were in disguise, but you were asking questions about Sally. I had already read the note that was in Sally's handbag, and I had just discovered what lay under that wagonload of garbage in the alley."

"Hmm. But how'd you know it was me, through my disguise, I mean?"

"As I said, I have a knack "

"Right." Thomas's face lit up in a broad grin. "For seeing through disguises. Well, here's some advice. You might think twice before letting certain people, especially a certain young person, know about that trait of yours. This particular person loathes being laughed at. He'd make a very bad adversary, I think."

"I'll remember that, Thomas. Thank you. And here's some advice for you, as well. You and your Uncle Edward might try to find out, by whatever methods you usually employ, exactly who at Marshalsea Prison was the intended recipient of that note in Sally's handbag. Tie up the last of the loose ends, so to speak."

Thomas gave Will a salute, opened the door and departed again. The room was eerily quiet for a few moments, but I made no move. In that dark niche carved into Lord Wotton's library wall, with no other sound than the pounding of my heart, the last piece of the puzzle came to me, and I knew that Will was wrong. Finding out who the note was intended for would not tie up the last loose end. No matter what they believed in their smug, male minds, Father and Thomas and Henry—and even Will—did not have all the answers to this mystery. But I did. And Father had given me the clue.

"Is it safe now?" I whispered.

"I make no guarantees," Will said, folding his arms and keeping his gaze on the door.

My fingers lifted the tapestry. "I don't care," I said, bursting from the niche. "There's something I must tell you."

The tight quarters had been damaging to my skirt. It billowed and flounced all around me. When I reached the center of the room, I bent to smooth out several wrinkles and glanced up to see Will's eyes following my moves. He appeared not to have a care in the world. Like Father and Thomas and Henry, he believed the mystery was solved. His gaze traveled up my form and stopped at my face.

"You must feel terribly clever now," I said.

Will reached up to twirl his earring.

"Your brother Luke used that word yesterday. He said I seemed very clever. He does that often, attempting to manipulate me. It's quite humorous, really. He was trying to trick me into helping him find Sally."

"And it worked," I broke in. "You found Sally, and you prevented the Queen's assassination. You both did it, even though you got all the credit." I lowered my voice. "But you still don't know the really important part, the dangerous part."

"What do you mean?"

"You know that Sally carried the note in her handbag. You know the note was meant for someone at Marshalsea Prison, but—" I paused dramatically, "you have no idea who wrote the note."

"And I suppose you do." Will only cocked an eyebrow, but he seemed to be laughing at me. Who was I, he must be wondering, to think I could unravel this plot? I raised myself to my full height.

"Luke told me about your play, the comedy you're writing. He told me you reduced the action to one simple idea: mistaken identity."

"Yes, but what's that got to do with it?"

"It has everything to do with it. I mistook the identity of our mastermind, and the word *clever* made me realize it. You heard it, too. My father said that Maines, the man we knew as Basset, did not seem clever enough to have devised the plot against the Queen. So, if Father was right, if it was not Basset, then it was someone else."

He rolled his eyes. "Your logic is impeccable. Have you figured out the identity of this someone else?"

"I think so. The mastermind is someone at your theater, someone who knew Thomas would be there for my audition, someone who believed Thomas was in love with Sally and that he would look for her. That same person did not want Thomas tracking down a dead girl and finding her murderer. So he sent Patrick and Jack to follow Thomas and kill him."

"There are at least a dozen men in the troupe. Have you narrowed the list to one?"

I nodded. "Gilbert Dereham."

Will laughed aloud. "I cannot abide the man's company, but that's no reason to accuse him of treason. I hope you'll give me a better reason to believe you."

"I can give you four, but I must convince you quickly. Once Gilbert realizes that Basset and the others are captured, then he will try to kill the Queen on his own. At the theater yesterday," I said, holding one finger aloft, "Gilbert eavesdropped on Thomas and Arthur's conversation about Sally. Why would he have done that, except to find out how much Thomas knew?"

"That's easy. Because he's an obnoxious boor. You saw how he insisted on revealing my life story to everyone on stage, the fact that I came from Stratford, that I have twins. The man is an ass," he added with a grin, "but that doesn't make him an assassin."

"Here's the second one, then." I held up another finger. "Gilbert fancies himself a writer. You recall he claimed as much when the other actors made him believe they were about to produce a play in Latin. So, he could have written the note, with its reversed spelling of the Queen's name and the hidden symbolism that the hope of the future will shoot forth from amidst the offal."

"True enough," he said, "but any writer might have written such a note."

Undeterred, I held up a third finger. "Just now in the banquet hall, Basset told the men to wait for the signal. Not his signal, I realize now, but the signal. When it came, I was right there, but I missed it."

Will stifled a yawn.

"You might have missed it, too," I went on. "When Lord Wotton proposed a toast to the Queen, Basset was passing by Gilbert Dereham's chair with a tray of glasses. Gilbert took a glass from Basset's tray and announced that today was April the twenty-fourth, the Eve of St. Mark's. And then he said, 'You may go,' almost as if he were a lord. Brooke and Ellen laughed at him, and I just dismissed him as drunk. But immediately after that, Basset told Toby that it was time to go."

"Those reasons are plausible," Will admitted, folding his arms as if bored, "but hardly enough to convict a man of treason."

I grinned widely. "My last reason is why you cannot abide his company. Gilbert enjoys showing off his superior knowledge, especially of Greek and Latin. I believe that he combined two Latin words and then turned them into an English word in order to make fun of his uneducated followers. Each time he heard them say the word he must have had a great laugh at their ignorance."

Will unfolded his arms. "Which Latin words? Which English word?"

"The English word is *rosemary*. Patrick used that word as the reason he planned to kill Luke yesterday morning. The Latin words are *rosa* and *mori.*"

"The rose must die!" Will broke in. "The Tudor rose, Elizabeth."

"Precisely. Basset called her the bastard rose. Luke told me he used the phrase *memento mori*—remember, you must die—when he entertained you with the story about our great-uncle who lost his head over Queen Katherine."

Will was staring into the distance, hardly seeming to listen. I took a step toward him. "I would suppose that Gilbert's huge, bejeweled hands could inflict quite a lot of damage. Have you wondered who gave Basset that black eye?"

"Because Basset killed Sally, you think?" He brought his gaze back to me. "But you still have given no motive for Gilbert to want the Queen dead."

"You're right. I haven't figured out a motive, but you told me yourself that temperament is more important than motive. Ten people might have motive, you said, but only one of them might have the temperament to commit murder."

"And why do you think Gilbert has the necessary temperament?"

I shrugged. "Call it a woman's second sight. I think I loathe him as much as you do, and all because he said female actors were a sacrilege and a horror."

"Female," Will repeated. He snapped his fingers. "A woman may be the clue to Gilbert Dereham's motive, but not the woman you think. You stay here. I have to find Thomas."

And he was gone, slamming the door behind him.

"Stay here?" I yelled to the empty room. "I'm supposed to stay here while you go out and catch Gilbert and get all my glory?" Furious, I picked up my skirts and ran after him. But I had forgotten about the blasted ottoman.

When I finally rolled to a stop next to the wall, I had lost my shoes and my hair ribbons. I sat up, tears streaming down my face.

"Well, that's just lovely!" I said between sobs. "No wonder men have the best roles in theater. Their clothes don't get in the way."

The door creaked just then, and I wiped at my face. Will can't see me like this, I thought and pulled my skirt close around me. I had landed behind Lord Wotton's chair, so perhaps he would not see me at all.

But it was not Will.

Gilbert Dereham tiptoed into the room.

The same instinct that had made me silently follow Will this morning caused me to keep silent now. Hardly daring to blink, I watched as Gilbert closed the door. He crept to the center of the room and came to a stop in front of the ottoman. Somehow, the little footstool had managed to remain upright, though its top lay across the room. For several moments, Gilbert stood very still and studied the contents of the ottoman. Seemingly satisfied, he moved stealthily and very steadily to the window.

He pulled the drape aside a fraction of an inch and peered outside, but only for an instant. The drape fell from his hand, and he let out a ragged sigh as if in deep distress.

My thoughts raced feverishly. I needed a plan. And I had very little time. Right now, Gilbert did not suspect that I was here, but any minute he would glance in my direction.

What should I do? There seemed to be nothing I could do.

Will's words came back to me: *It's like being in a play that the author hasn't quite finished writing yet.*

Yes, I thought, *this scene is exactly like that.* And then I realized something about Will's description. The writer was the one with the power. There was something I could do, after all. I could pretend that I did not know Gilbert was in the room.

Quietly at first, and then a bit louder and a bit louder still, I began to sob. Heart-breaking sobs. I was not sure when he heard me or caught sight of me. I was holding the skirt of my dress to my eyes when I was aware that he stood over me. I lifted my face. His massive form was blurred.

"Go away," I said, hiccuping and breaking into more sobs.

214

"What are you doing here?" His voice was low, menacing.

"I'm hiding," I sniffed. "From Lord Wotton."

He studied me for several long moments. "You look like that little actor fellow from the theater." He snapped his fingers. "You're Thomas's cousin, aren't you?" His hand went to his sword hilt. "Why are you in a woman's costume?"

"Because I am a woman," I replied. "I'm Luke's sister, Lucy. His twin sister. And I wish I'd stayed home. Lord Wotton won't keep his hands off me. Help me up," I said, giving him my hand. To my surprise and relief, he pulled me to my feet. His eyes traveled down my figure, and he reached for my waist. I wiggled from his grasp and strode past him, as if I had nothing to be afraid of, moving in the general direction of the window.

I reached the wall before I heard his heavy step behind me. I put out my hand for the drape.

"Don't," he said, gripping my wrist. "You never know who might be watching."

His huge frame towered over me. I was close enough to smell his breath and detected not a trace of ale. Gilbert was a very good actor.

"It's warm in here," I said. "I just wanted some air."

He tapped his sword hilt. "Touch that drape again, and I'll open your throat instead of the window.

I laughed nervously. "You're not serious?"

"Try me."

He dropped my wrist, and I shrank back against the book-shelves. "You wouldn't," I whispered, my hands at my throat. And it was in that moment, frightened and face-to-face with the very man who wanted to kill the Queen, that I knew the truth about Gilbert Dereham. The same truth that Will must have realized only moments before. "You're just like me," I said.

His eyes narrowed to slits. "What?"

"Your family was disgraced," I said, so nervous I could barely hear my own words. "Just like mine. My great-uncle, Thomas Culpeper, committed adultery with the wife of old King Henry. He was beheaded. His head hung on a pike above the great bridge."

A glimmer of a smile lit up his eyes, but I felt no less endangered. I took a breath and went on. "An ancestor of yours, Francis Dereham, did the same thing, and the king had him drawn and quartered. This," I finished, my voice stronger, "this is why you hate the Queen. She is old Henry's daughter."

He shrugged. He held my gaze a moment longer. Then, turning his head away the slightest bit, he did what he had told me not to do, he pulled the drape aside and peered out. At most, I had two or three seconds. My hands moved past my throat to the shelf directly behind me and closed around an object, so cool to the touch that I shivered. In one motion, I lifted the object and brought it crashing down on the back of Gilbert's head, and he crumpled to the floor. Immediately, a rather satisfying amount of blood began staining his collar a bright red.

"Thank you, Homer," I said to the small, marble sculpture. With hands that were only just now beginning to shake, I put the blind old soul back into his place next to Lord Wotton's copy of *The Odyssey*.

The door opened, and in walked Will, rubbing his hands together precisely as Father had done earlier.

"It's all taken care of," he said.

"What's taken care of?" I asked, stepping over Gilbert and rushing forward.

"Thomas has set soldiers on guard around the house. The villain can't escape now." Will pulled on his mustache. "You'll remember that I concluded the note we found in Sally's handbag possessed neither rhyme nor reason. Well, it still has no rhyme," he said with a grin, "but we definitely discerned its reason, did we not?"

I opened my mouth to disagree, but I caught myself just in time. "Luke deciphered most of it," I said, but I don't think Will heard me. He was tapping his chin, as if deep in thought.

"Thomas told me that Patrick has made a confession. It seems Gilbert talked often about the humiliation of having a woman on the English throne. Patrick hasn't said yet which nobleman Gilbert planned to replace her with, but I'm sure Sir Francis can get that out of him."

"Well," I said, "that goes along with Gilbert's disapproval of female actors, doesn't it?"

217

Will still seemed to be deep in his own thoughts. "Gilbert's vanity matches his girth," he said. "The man set quite a store by his knowledge of Latin."

"And Greek," I broke in.

"And Greek. He was very patronizing to those whom he considered beneath his level of education. I can't forget how he tried to humiliate me in front of the entire troupe. Well, once the soldiers find him, he won't be laughing anymore. The wretched fellow lived by his University pedigree, by his superior knowledge of Latin, and it was Latin that did him in."

"I really think it was Greek."

"What?"

"To be exact, it was Homer," I said, angling my head to the rear wall where one could just see Gilbert's head behind a chair. By now, his collar was a dark shade of red.

Will leaned forward. "Is he dead?"

I shrugged. "I don't know."

"If he isn't, then he soon will be. Sir Francis will see to it that he's drawn and quartered."

I looked up, with more than a mild curiosity. "Do you really think so?"

"Of course. The man was planning to assassinate the Queen. They don't just slap your wrist for that."

"Yes!" I shouted, and did a little dance, clapping my hands above my head. "Now your troupe definitely has an opening. Mr. Bright will *have* to hire...that is," I caught

218

myself just in time. "Luke will certainly get a job there now."

"Tell me something…Lucy," Will said.

I glanced up from my impromptu jig. His dark eyes were studying me, and I stood very still. Several moments passed, and I held my breath, certain he had guessed the truth.

"What?" I finally said.

"Just now, how did you manage to overcome Gilbert Dereham? Be quick. See if you can tell me in a word or two," he added.

I clasped my hands demurely at my waist. "I made him believe I was helpless."

Will continued to stare at me. "Perhaps I'm wrong," he began. "Perhaps I shouldn't say this," he went on and bit his lip as if reluctant to finish.

He knows the truth, I thought, and my spirits sagged. *What gave me away?*

His dark, intelligent eyes narrowed. "I'm going to tell you something, something you may not want to share with Luke. But I think you may be a better actor than your brother."

I opened my mouth to laugh, but I was so relieved that the sound came out like a gasp. "Then it's a shame, isn't it?" I said. "A shame I'll never get to act on the British stage."

"Oh, I wouldn't bet on that," he said, reaching up to twirl the golden hoop in his ear. "If anyone could manage that feat, it's you, Lucy. I'm sure you'll find a way."

I held his gaze a moment. "Thank you, sir. Your flattery means a great deal."

He shook his head. "Oh, 'twas not flattery. Luke is the one who flatters, remember?"

"And speaking of Luke," I broke in, "I think it's time to practice a bit of stagecraft he taught me." With a nod, I turned and walked to the door. "The dramatic exit," I said as I faced him again, making a curtsey, as pretty as any I had made on-stage that afternoon.

"Perhaps we'll see each other again," he said.

"I doubt that, sir. I lead a very sheltered life. My brother has all the fun."

"Well, then, may he have many adventures to report to you." He made a low bow. "Good night, Lady Lucinda."

"Good night, Mr. Shakespeare."

As I closed the door, my last glimpse was of the smile curling his lips. Yes, indeed, I thought. May Luke have many, many adventures, and I would not object in the least if they involved the roguishly handsome Mr. Shakespeare.